The Quality of Light

The Quality of Light

Richard Collins

SEREN

Seren is the book imprint of
Poetry Wales Press Ltd
57 Nolton Street, Bridgend, Wales, CF31 3AE
www.serenbooks.com

ISBN 978-1-85411-536-2

A CIP record for this title is available from the British Library.

This book is a work of fiction. Like most fiction it is taken from life; for this
reason names and details of characters have been altered to protect actual
persons.

Cover photograph © Lotte Lodge 2010

Inner design and typesetting by books@lloydrobson.com

Printed by Short Run Press, Exeter

The publisher works with the financial assistance of
the Welsh Books Council.

One

The city looks good. In front of him is a stretch of tideless water, the floating harbour, and beyond that, handsome old buildings and handsome new ones, catching the morning sun. But the tallest and most beautiful structures are the temporary ones: six red cranes standing above a half-constructed complex of steel and concrete, their shapes outlined against the sky. At the moment two of them are moving while the others stand still and wait their turn. He watches them lift and swing and lower their loads into place. He looks at the nearest crane and his eyes follow the metal ladders that lead up to the cab. It's a long climb; he thinks the crane driver must stay up there, high above the city, for the whole day. Now three of the cranes are turning at the same time, two clockwise, one anti-clockwise. A slow mechanical dance. A meeting of form and function. Better than art.

Daniel has come to this side of the water to a building known simply as the Gallery. It is a converted warehouse, four storeys high, an art centre with exhibitions, a cafe and a bookshop. He walks around the sculpture that stands between the building and the edge of the harbour. It is a large, solidly made steel bottle resting on its side. It has portholes like a ship and Daniel looks in, as he did once before. Inside is a cabin with a bed, a fitted wardrobe and chest of drawers, a table and a chair; everything made of stainless steel. It is dimly lit and therefore appears monochrome, like an old photograph. He walks around and looks through the opposite porthole. He stands back and reads a plaque bearing the name of the work: *The Voyage*. On each side of the sculpture stands a tree, a little incongruous here, perhaps pointing up the change in the landscape from industrial to post-industrial. And there is a wooden bench to sit on and look at the view of the city. Daniel resists the temptation and goes into the building.

The place has just opened for the day and he is the only visitor. In the foyer a young woman in a Gallery T-shirt pushes a vacuum cleaner. Two men come through carrying a piece of what looks like stage scenery. Daniel climbs the stairs to the second floor and enters an exhibition space. On the walls are photographs of the city taken twenty or thirty years ago. They are stylish pictures, many of them well composed. They all feature people caught unawares, sometimes in the foreground, sometimes further away, ordinary people in ordinary moments, fragments of past lives. Down one side of the gallery is a series of photographs taken in a park, the trees all bending a little in the wind. He looks at each photograph in turn until, halfway along the wall, he comes to a window.

He looks out through the dirty glass at trees motionless in still air. Down below is the sculpture, the large bottle. A man and a woman walk around and look in through the portholes. There is something in their body language that suggests an awareness of each other's presence, a mutual geography. Daniel is alone in the gallery and it is silent. He hears these words: 'I'm glad you're here.'

'Yes.'

'You're a good friend.'

Nobody has spoken.

He watches the couple move away, the man looking across the water to the city, the woman looking down at the ground in front of her as if lost in thought. Daniel knows this is real time. It looks like memory.

He leaves the exhibition and goes downstairs to the first floor. On the wall hangs a large hand-drawn map of a city, perhaps this city. But all the streets are named after what seem to be states of mind: Melancholy Avenue leads to Desolation Road; Ecstatic Avenue is close to Serenity Square; Contemplative Crescent runs off Jolly Street. It appears to be a place of conflicting emotions. In the middle of the room there are some small, intricately detailed model villages and towns and industrial buildings made of paper and set on rough old pieces of plywood. Each tiny house or church or shopping precinct is finely made. He makes journeys through these miniature landscapes by letting his eyes wander at random. The last model he looks at is the one near the exit. An eight-by-four sheet of ply makes a vast landscape with a small community of houses at one end. Far away, at the opposite end of the sheet, is a minute tent standing on its own. It is only a model made of wood and paper but Daniel inhabits this landscape for a moment. He feels very much alone.

A particular place will arouse particular thoughts and feelings. He knows this is true. Or perhaps he projects his feelings onto what he sees. He remembers some words that were spoken when he was in this place before, many years ago. It was the first evening of the course, or *the project*, as it was called. They had gathered together on the top floor of the art centre in a room not normally open to the public. The man leading the course (Daniel can't remember his name now) had given out an itinerary for the five days, explained some of his ideas, talked about what might be achieved. Then he switched off the lights and gave a slide show with commentary: some famous and not so famous paintings that might influence them. Daniel remembers the picture of floppy watches in a surreal landscape, sea cliffs in the background. And some not quite abstract mountain scenes. And a bright cheerful painting in reds, blues and yellows depicting a foreign city, Moscow perhaps, or was it St Petersburg? The picture showed a hotchpotch of colourful buildings under a sky full of birds and clouds and sunshine. It looked like a happy place. Daniel remembers the words the man used to describe this painting, the last one they were shown.

'The city is mindstuff,' he said. 'One part memory and one part imagination.'

Daniel is a tall man in his early thirties. He has a slim, athletic build but his face is a little worn and faded by experience; he isn't a *young* man any more. He has short hair but is scruffily dressed, is tanned from a summer of working out of doors, moves gracefully. He has been to this city only once before in his life. He stayed for a few days some six years ago and hasn't come back until now.

Daniel comes out of the door of the art centre and walks to the edge of the docks. The water is a dirty brown colour but its surface catches the sunlight and shines silver and blue. A ferry passes, its bow wave spreading in a V shape and eventually lapping against the stonework by his feet. On the other side of the water the city spreads up over the low hills, the buildings making jagged shapes against the skyline. Shiny office blocks congregate in the lower part of town. Limestone mansions sit up on the heights. There are church spires new and old. And, of course there are the cranes: the six red cranes, a group of green ones further away, and on this side of the water two retired, grey, dockside cranes that were once used to unload ships. He walks up to one of them now and allows his eyes to take him up the metal framework and out above the water. He moves on.

Where the docks narrow he comes to a bridge that carries two lanes of clattering traffic and a footpath across the water. He makes his way across the bridge and follows the road into a busy part of the city, takes a random left turn, a right, passes through a small square. He is in the business district and people are moving fast about their workday activities. Daniel walks slowly and looks at blank city faces, at fake stone facades, at discarded burger wrappers in dirty gutters, at patches of blue sky framed by the shapes of buildings. It's OK; the city is a novelty. He lives in a small town in the hills far away, he works outdoors in the countryside, this is something different. And it is a bright morning, the air is clear, the city looks beautiful to him. A friend of a friend offered him an empty house to stay in for a few days; all he has to do is feed the cat. So he came. He needed to get away.

He tries to think what it was he wanted to get away from. It was a small thing, an overheard conversation. Daniel has a new girlfriend, Sarah, a woman of his own age. They have been seeing each other for six months and they have good times together. And there is the child, a bright little girl of two and a half years, lots of fun to be with; not his child but he is fond of her; how could he not be? And it is a rainy day and he is laid off from work and lets himself into the house that he spends more and more time in nowadays. The place is empty. He makes tea, takes it into the living room and falls asleep on the sofa. He wakes to overhear an ordinary conversation: 'They're having a big wedding, an outdoor ceremony, live music under the trees...' It's a woman's voice, a friend of Sarah's. 'And she's very happy to be settling down at last.'

'I didn't think she cared for him that much. That's what she told me before,' Sarah says.

'No. Well, she's fond of him. I mean, she's wanted to settle down and have a child for so long,' the friend says. 'He's a good guy – very reliable. OK, maybe she doesn't really passionately love him and all that. But, you know. It's the right time for her.'

A little pause. The sound of rain against the window. Daniel keeps his eyes shut in case Sarah comes in and finds him there.

Then it's Sarah's voice: 'It's like that with me and Dan. He's good with Elly. It's not a deep, passionate thing but he's getting to be part of the family. I trust him.' There's a tiny pause now and a change of subject. 'Hey, did I tell you about Elly's nursery school teacher, the one that looks like a film star?'

He takes a left into a narrow cobbled street with smaller old buildings on each side. Red brick. Sandstone. Flaking layers of paint and crumbling plaster. Brick again.

It's not a deep passionate thing but he's getting to be part of the family. What's the big deal? The big deal is this: he hasn't heard women discuss relationships in that way before, so straightforwardly practical, so unromantic. Like the way you would choose a car: *it's not sporty but it does fifty miles to the gallon. It is reliable and has low maintenance costs.*

He feels foolish for being so affected by it. It's not a big deal but he'd imagined that she would speak of him with a little more enthusiasm. And he thought that relationships might be something more than that. But he's thirty-two for God's sake, he's a grown-up. It's not such a big thing.

Sarah had come into the living room and wiggled his foot. He had to pretend to wake up. 'Hello, trouble,' she said. 'You're home then.' She smiled and it seemed like nothing had happened. It hadn't. And then he came here to this city of all places.

When he was here before, they did some pretentious nonsense. A random walk with a French name, *la dérive*. They spoke as if a walk in the city was of profound philosophical consequence, a subversive act. He is doing the random thing now, he thinks. He follows a winding alleyway between stone walls topped with broken glass. It leads to a busy four-lane road with a stretch of the harbour on the other side. The harbour again; he must have walked in a sort of loop.

Traffic fumes and traffic noise and voices in his head. He remembers that first evening when they had to introduce themselves and explain why they were there. Everyone sitting around a big table, each person not listening properly to the others because they were preparing themselves for their own turn. There was a film-maker, a nice, straightforward man who filmed pavements and legs and feet. There was a woman who painted maps of psychic energy in the landscape and who talked about the aborigines. There were two middle-aged landscape painters and a philosopher poet in a long leather coat. There were others who he can't remember now. And there was one person who was very important to him at that time.

When it came to his turn he had said: 'I'm not sure why I'm here, really,' and as he spoke he thought: *I am here because she is here.* Then he realised that everybody in the room knew that. 'I like looking at things,' he said. 'I just do.'

The man leading the project was called Michael, there, he remembers his name now. Michael said something encouraging about the importance of observation. All art starts with observation.

Then it was her turn and she said something about her poems connecting people with places. She talked about point of view, something about the character of the person being superimposed on the landscape. She was so serious and so wonderful. He remembers and he smiles.

There is a possible gap in the traffic and he dashes across all four lanes. A lorry hoots at him. He walks to the water's edge, turns, and heads towards the locks at the end of the harbour. He walks with the water on one side of him and the busy road on the other. The harbour is a historical relic now, even more so than when he was here before. There is no commercial shipping here at all; this morning the only craft on the water are a flotilla of tiny one-person sailing boats. And they aren't doing much as there is little wind.

The road and the docks part company and Daniel chooses to follow the water's edge. He walks past metal sheds, some of them abandoned, some occupied by small businesses: a furniture maker, an importer of oriental rugs, a boat builder. There are disused railway lines set in the concrete, cast-iron bollards to which big ships were once tied up, old, rusted pieces of engine, stacks of wooden pallets. He walks past a derelict warehouse in a sea of broken glass and abandoned household waste.

His walk isn't random any more; he realises that. For now he has a destination and he moves purposefully towards it. He less than half recognises his surroundings, his mental map of the city is full of holes, but he goes on. There is a place he wants to see. Attached to that place is a fragment of memory.

Traffic again, roads coming in from different directions and meeting in a complicated junction by a larger body of water. A car park, a grassy area, an ugly new cafe. He passes below a flyover that he knows is actually a huge, rarely opened, swing bridge. And here the view opens out. He walks onto a promontory between two sets of locks and stands at what looks like the edge of the city. On his right old houses climb the hill to a flat summit occupied by the handsome limestone terraces and mansions. On his left, across the river, are allotments and a deer park and green suburbs. In front of him the river, really an estuary here, flows away through a high-sided gorge towards the sea. It is low tide and the mud glistens in the sunshine.

There is tarmac. There is stone. There are trees on the riverbank showing the first touches of autumn colour. Massive timbers are stacked in a pile. A rusted chain is coiled next to a wooden bollard. Behind him big lorries drive across the swing bridge and fill the air with fumes and noise. There is a beauty to it all, he feels. And a good vigorous pulsing of weekday life.

He hears words again, just ordinary words: 'I'm glad you're here.'

'Yes.'

'You're a good friend.'

She had been pointing something out to him, a building

on the skyline perhaps, or a bird flying overhead; he can't remember. She had turned to him and touched his bare forearm with her fingertips and pointed at something and then their eyes had caught for a moment before she looked away and spoke. It was a long time ago and it is now.

This city. He has memories so strongly attached to this place that they feel like something more than merely personal associations, they are the qualities of the place itself, objectively true. And he knows that there are other people for whom this place has meanings and memories as vivid as his own. Others will stand here or move about the city carrying their own stories with them. He tries to think of that, the huge extra dimension of mindstuff resting on the landscape, layer upon layer of thoughts and memories. It is more than he can imagine.

Two

The south side of the city; a less attractive area. Michael walks along a street that follows the top of a low ridge. There are only houses, terrace after terrace of red-brick, Victorian, bow-fronted and flat-fronted respectable little houses. The only time there is something worth looking at is when he passes a junction of a road that leads downhill towards the water and the centre of town. Each junction makes a gap in the buildings through which he can look at a view of the city.

Michael is a sturdy middle-aged man with a broad face, salt-and-pepper stubble on his chin, thick grey hair. He walks with a limp; his right leg drags a little. He is somewhat lop-sided and unsteady but he moves briskly; he's not unfit. He is thinking about a dream.

It wasn't last night but the night before that he had dreamt Zoë had come home. 'Hi, Dad. Is it alright if I stay for a while?' she said. She reached up and kissed him on the cheek.

That was it. Not much of a dream but he had been unable to get back to sleep. He had gone downstairs, lit the fire and started looking at old photographs. And then, in the middle of the night, he started a new painting. He had worked on it for a couple of hours, gone back to bed for an hour before dawn, got up and spent most of the day working on it again until it was pretty much finished.

He comes to a junction and a view: the spire of St Peter's, office blocks, multi-storey car parks and, because the city is renewing itself, brightly coloured cranes. He stops for a moment and takes it in. He walks on, thinking about the dream and thinking about the painting. It had been rather spontaneous but he seemed to know what he wanted to do. He had created a textured background by spreading brown and grey ink onto the canvas with a roller. He drew two figures in charcoal and then covered them over with pieces of torn newspaper to make their outlines less distinct. He redrew them. Then he experimented with horizontal strips of newspaper and horizontal stripes of rollered-on paint until the image was half-obscured, like something seen through dirty glass. Two figures sitting on a bench, a significant space between them and one of them turned away from the other. It was from an old photograph of himself and his wife, taken by Zoë just before they split up. The body language said everything. His painting captured the feeling of that moment and the sense of time having passed. It looked like memory.

He can't go out to work now; his health is too unpredictable for that. He has recently been diagnosed with a seriously bad-shit degenerative disease and his outlook is bleak. So he stays home and paints. He wants to do more memory pictures, a series of body language pieces from old photographs or perhaps from the imagination. If it comes off it will be an autobiography in paint, something for a small exhibition. He is a lonely middle-aged man whose ex-wife lives on the other side of the city and whose daughter lives far away. His health is bad. And yet this morning he is excited, he is painting again, he feels a sense of fulfilment. And it really is a beautiful day. He is almost happy.

He walks until he comes to another junction and this time turns and follows the road downhill, towards the city centre. The framed view in front of him is a little different from the last one: no St Peter's and not so many cranes but a glint of sunlight on water from the docks. And, on the hill opposite, a large white chimney that belongs to the hospital. He walks well going downhill, hardly limping at all; anyone would think there is nothing wrong with him. He looks out across the city and tries not to look up at the hospital. There are lots of other buildings on the skyline (the university physics department, the 1960s Catholic cathedral, the new passport offices – he knows them all) but his eyes will keep being drawn to the place that has recently become significant to him. The hospital chimney is probably something to do with the central heating, it only looks like they have a crematorium conveniently situated for the disposal of those who don't make it.

Michael sees a mental picture of the not-waving-but-drowning man, the one who was in the bed opposite him. The man was in a desperate condition, unable to walk, incontinent, speech blurred, mind wandering. And in the night Michael would wake and see him waving one pyjama-clad arm in the air like a flag, a distress signal. Michael decided to keep the curtains drawn around his bed rather than see this whenever he woke. It was a neurological ward and there were other disturbing cases, some of them worse than the not-waving man. In a separate room there stayed an unconscious young woman whose only sign of life was an occasional slightly less than human scream. The mood of the hospital staff and most of the patients was positive and upbeat despite everything. And so it must be; Michael himself had kept up a cheerful front during his stay there. But now, outdoors in the morning sunshine, he is touched by the memory of the screaming woman, the not-waving man, and some of the others.

At the bottom of the hill he comes to Canal Street. He walks along as far as a pedestrian crossing, waits for the lights, crosses and takes the steps up onto the footbridge above the canal. He walks to the middle of the bridge and looks out. The canal was built when the old course of the river was converted into a harbour with a permanent high tide. Now the river water flows down the canal and out through the gorge to the sea. And, when the tide is in, the seawater flows up the canal right into the dirty suburbs of the city.

When he first came out of hospital he couldn't sleep at night. He experienced little tremors in his back and his limbs that kept him awake and in a state of anxiety. So he would get up and walk through the silent streets down to the canal to see the water. Some nights he would come down here two or three times, look at the moon coming out from behind the clouds, look at the tide coming up into the city, and feel that the world was still turning. It was some sort of comfort.

He looks down from the bridge now. The tide is out and the water flows fast and muddy. Along the banks of the canal the trees (ash, sycamore and also fig trees – no one knows why) have already started to change colour, greens fading to yellow. He moves on.

Michael has lived in this city for more than two decades and the landscape of the place had become invisible to him. But something has happened since his illness took hold. Perhaps it is no more than the fact that he spent two weeks on a hospital ward waiting for tests and results, and when he was free to go out into the world again it looked different. Perhaps it is the fact that he has some bad days when he does nothing and goes nowhere and that makes the good days, the ones when he feels well, more special than they would otherwise be. Or is it his new awareness of the limits of his existence, the sense that his time is circumscribed? Whatever it is, the world does look brighter and more interesting. And it is a new season now; the dirty hot days of summer are over. There has been a change in the quality of light.

Now he walks down a road that takes him along the boundary of the defunct dockside timber yards. Every possible sort of wall and fence in every possible state of decay and renewal is found here, all the richness of their colours and textures lit by a low autumn sun. Old red bricks, pitted and worn, mortar crumbling, flecked with white paint from an advertisement that faded long ago. Grey and brown sandstone, eroded in lines that follow ancient bedding planes. Triangular copes made of black and purple slag left over from the steel-making days. Railway sleepers oozing tar. New concrete blocks, rusted corrugated iron, sheets of asbestos. It is an exhibition in an outdoor gallery.

Michael crosses a large car park, empty except for two lorries, and goes up the steps into a cafe. He goes to the counter, buys a coffee, spills much of it as he limps across to a table by the window. He likes cafes. He enjoys the fact that he can be anonymous and alone and at the same time experience some of the warmth and *bonhomie* of people gathered together. He likes to visit a whole load of different cafes around the city and take in the atmosphere of each one.

Now he looks out of the window, across the car park and the dock basin, and at the houses running up the hill. He looks across a patch of grass to the swing bridge with its flow of traffic. He drinks his coffee and thinks some more about photographs.

He has been looking at photographs of himself taken so long ago that he can hardly remember being that person. The things that mattered to him, his motivations, his thoughts, his sense of self, all has changed. That's how it seems to him now. He has looked at pictures of himself as young layabout, a lover, teacher, family man. Roles he can no longer play. He doesn't want to think about who he can be now. Except that he continues to be an artist, that's good. It's something. The funny thing is that in many of the photographs he is recognisably himself, Michael Marantz. His outer form remains somewhat the same. His body is a shell, he thinks, a house that has been occupied by many different people, each one moving on and leaving just a few things behind.

The windows of the cafe have been cleaned recently but the job has been done in a hurry and thick dirty horizontal smears have been left behind. Michael looks out through the dirt at a young man walking across the car park. The man makes his way to the edge of the docks, turns, and walks on until he passes out of sight under the swing bridge. Michael thinks that this illness has an effect on his mind; he finds himself mistaking strangers in the street for people he once knew. Sometimes he will move as if to greet someone and then turn away when he realises that he has got it wrong again. It can be embarrassing. The dreamy young man disappearing under the swing bridge, for example. He looks like someone Michael once knew. It was some time ago.

Three

Something has happened, perhaps an accident, and the traffic has come to a standstill half a mile from the end of the motorway link into the city. It gives Isabel time to collect her thoughts. Here she is in her new (or nearly new) red Peugeot; smartly dressed (an expensive sweater, short skirt over woollen tights, city shoes), a young professional woman starting afresh. She will be in the city for a few days, maybe all week, and she will try to find a small house to buy. She believes her future is here. It's good.

The traffic is easing forward on her left, a gap opens up and she steers into it, creeps along for a few yards, comes to a standstill again. There are advertising hoardings on one side of the road and warehouses on the other. Ahead of her she can see office blocks, some red cranes, a church spire, the university buildings on the hill – everything lit by a low autumn sun. But Isabel is impatient; she thought that her arrival in the city would be brisk and businesslike. Now she turns on the radio and tunes it to a local station. The weather, she hears, will be sunny but not particularly hot, outlook changeable, some showers ahead. She turns the radio off and tries to think of her new life here. She is a radiologist, recently trained, and this will be her second job, a long-term appointment. It is a worthwhile career, pays well, and she can be comfortable and independent. When she was here before she was a little crazy, an idealist, a poet. Yes, she actually thought of herself as a poet. Well, it was a long time ago. Now she has grown up.

The traffic begins to move forward again and she lifts her foot off the clutch and follows, picks up a little speed, changes into second, now third. She can see the lights of the junction ahead and lets out a small sigh of relief. It's stop and go up to the lights and then things are a little easier. She follows signs to a car park and takes a ticket at the barrier. Soon she is out of the car and on foot, setting off into the city and into her future.

She walks through a characterless shopping precinct that seems to go on and on until, at last, she comes to a wide street that leads up to the classier end of town. Here she relaxes, takes her time, and practises being herself, Isabel Davies, the sophisticated city woman, looking in shop windows. The street is good; all the buildings come from an earlier time and look distinguished, their limestone recently cleaned up. There is a sense of prosperity here, both past and present. She passes a music shop with a window display of eccentric old stringed instruments. Then a large bookshop that she is tempted to go into; maybe it has a good poetry section. Then a place that sells upmarket ethnic clothing, not quite her scene now but she is nearly drawn in. Next door is a cafe called Primary Colours, furnished and decorated in black and white, with lots of chrome and mirrors. She glances in at the clientele – university lecturers and hip-capitalists, she thinks, and moves on. Further up the street she finds the estate agents; good, she thought she remembered there being one here. She looks in the window at the pictures of grand houses and suburban semis and little ordinary terraced houses selling at more than ordinary prices. She feels nervous but she pulls herself together, opens the door and goes in.

Now Isabel is a little further up the street, sitting in a cafe called The Ferry; it's more down to earth and less pretentious than the other one, she thinks. Spread on the table in front of her are some print-outs of cheaper, but not really cheap, properties. She has made pencil marks on some of them, underlining their good points and bad points. A half-drunk and now cold cup of coffee stands to one side. Isabel is staring into space and thinking about the word *home*. A house is just a house but a home sounds like somewhere that might be shared with other people. A family, for instance. This, she has to admit to herself, is sort of mental no-go area. Family. Children. She pushes the printouts into a neat pile with the most promising one on the top.

She has been nurturing an image of herself as an independent, emotionally strong woman. Tied to no one. In her past she has been in relationships with guys who wanted too much. The words from a song always come to mind when she thinks of this stuff, *I gave her my heart but she wanted my soul*, something like that, maybe it's an old Dylan number. Except that he was wrong, of course, that's not what women ask for, it's men that do that. They want too much. They want your soul. She's been caught like that more than once.

But then there was her most recent boyfriend. He didn't last very long at all because he wanted too little and didn't give very much either. So now she's free and independent for a while and that's good. That's how she wants to be. And then she is confronted by this word. *Home.*

Isabel looks out of the window and watches people passing by on the street. Today she is most interested in the women. The roles they play. She watches a stressed-out young mother with two toddlers in a double buggy. A happier mum, a three or four year old by her side, full of silly conversation and laughter, lots of smiles. Now there comes a smartly dressed business woman, high self-regard and serious purpose. Now, a young woman who might be a student, well dressed in a scruffy sort of way, sexy, something of the hedonistic wild-child about her. Isabel knows this person; she has been there and it was fun. And all the who-am-I-today-who-will-I-be-tomorrow uncertainty was exciting. But she would like to be more certain of herself now. She feels, for a moment, that she has lost the sense of who she really is. It's scary. She wishes that there was someone here to talk to.

Isabel is in the car again, driving around narrow streets. This whole hillside is covered with terraces of small houses. No shops, no open spaces, just houses. She has a map open on the seat beside her and stops from time to time to look at street names. When she finds the street she is looking for, there are no parking spaces and she must drive around in ever-widening circles until she can find somewhere to stop. She walks to the house, trying to imagine herself living in this area. She attempts to recapture the mental image she had of herself in this place. Who will she be here? Why is she doing this? Oh yes, she wants to exchange small-town life for big-city life, that's it. Theatre, films, dance, gigs, art galleries, expensive shops, fine architecture. It all seems rather wonderful. Or perhaps rather empty. Like treading water.

She finds number sixty-two and rings the bell. An overweight, unshaven man lets her in. He is friendly and polite. They start at the top; three tiny bedrooms, the world's smallest bathroom, new white paint over the damp patches, cheap fitted carpets. Downstairs to the kitchen, the dining room/living room. He is explaining the central heating system but Isabel begins to lose interest. She can hear an argument going on next door – a teenage girl and an older woman, her mother probably, are taking turns to shout at each other. They are speaking in a foreign language; Isabel thinks it must be Urdu or Bengali or something from that part of the world. A crash, as if a door has been slammed. More shouting, this time coming from close by, the combatants are standing a few feet away, separated from her only by a brick wall. The girl has changed to English and raises her voice. 'You stupid old cow,' she says, and then another door slams.

Isabel looks at the man. He is grinning; he has heard the same words.

'It's difficult for them,' he explains. 'They have such a huge generation gap.' He is a nice man, he is trying to understand. 'They are continents apart from each other. Worlds apart. On different planets.' He shrugs.

'I'll get back to you,' Isabel says.

'The price is negotiable,' he says.

She smiles but doesn't speak.

Isabel knows a few people in the city, old friends who she can drop in on when she comes here, friends with whom she can stay for a night or two. She hasn't seen Lucy for some years. She said she would visit her in the afternoon and it is not midday yet. But it would be good to talk to someone. She finds a parking space in Lucy's street, locks the car, walks a couple of hundred yards, rings the doorbell, composes herself.

Lucy opens the door and stands for a moment looking confused. 'Izzy, you look fantastic.' She leans forward and kisses Isabel on the cheek. 'Come in, come in. Do you want tea?' She turns her back and walks through to the kitchen. 'In here,' she calls over her shoulder.

Isabel follows, uncertain.

'It's a state, don't mind,' Lucy says. 'I've got some catching up to do.' She moves a pile of washing off a chair. 'Sit down.' She glances at Isabel but looks away again. Fills the electric kettle at the sink. When she finally faces Isabel her face wears a prepared smile. 'Wow, you look good. I like your hair like that.'

'I'm sorry,' Isabel says. 'I said I'd come this afternoon, didn't I? But I was in this part of town.' She tries not to see the domestic chaos. She notices that Lucy has put on weight, is unkempt, in a flap.

'It's OK,' Lucy says. 'I'm afraid I'm still catching up after the weekend.'

'I can come back later.'

'No way, Iz. Of course not. You'll just have to take me as you find me.' Lucy smiles some more. She turns away again and fiddles with the tea things. She brings two mugs and a packet of biscuits to the table, sits down opposite Isabel and waits for her to speak.

'Where's Jamie?' Isabel says.

'At school.'

'No!'

'Yes, he's five and a half. Five and three-quarters really. His birthday is in February.'

Isabel can't think what to say for a moment. She is aware

that the room holds twice as much furniture as it might do and that every surface is covered with debris, that's the word that comes into her mind. She is trying not to look around. She stirs her tea. Reaches for a biscuit; changes her mind. Wonders if this is how a room would look shortly after being hit by a flood or a tornado.

'You said you're buying a house,' Lucy says.

Isabel describes the house she has just visited. She says she won't be going back. There is another pause in the conversation and Lucy looks at her quizzically. 'You've reinvented yourself,' she says.

'It's only a haircut.'

'No, it's more than that. You look so smart.'

'It's a new me. It's who I want to be.' Isabel doesn't sound as sure as she would wish.

'You used to be, you know, a bit of a hippy. You were wild,' Lucy says. She looks like she's enjoying herself for a moment.

'I wasn't.'

'You used to take a lot of drugs.'

'I didn't. Not all the time. I suppose I was able to let myself go sometimes. I was young.'

'Well, I remember you getting pretty wrecked. You were wild, Iz.' Lucy smiles at the memory.

'That was a long time ago. I've changed. I've taken control of things. Anyway, I've always been this way inside.'

Lucy shakes her head.

'It's true,' Isabel says. 'This is the person I've always wanted to be.' She looks resigned rather than happy. 'I can't believe that Jamie is at school already. I thought he was still a toddler.'

'It's a bit of a relief.'

'Are you pleased to be back at work?'

Lucy nods. She is silent for a while. 'I had some trouble a while after Jamie,' she says. 'I never told you about it. I won't go into the details. It's just that I was desperate to have another baby but I couldn't any more. But I've got beautiful, wonderful Jamie. And Pete, of course. And still...' She looks up at Isabel, hoping for some sort of connection. 'I don't suppose you would be able to understand.'

'I don't know.' Isabel looks sympathetic. 'Are you and Pete alright?'

'He gets impatient with me. He wants... you know, it's important to men.'

There is a pause while Isabel tries to guess what she means. Then she speaks bluntly. 'It's important to women.'

'Yes, well.' Lucy is almost in tears. 'But tell me your stuff. Are you in a relationship?'

Isabel pauses before answering. 'I finished with someone recently. It was a sort of sex and friendship thing but without the friendship.'

'God.'

'It was alright. It was fun sometimes. But I'm glad it's over.' Isabel tries to think of something to say next. She begins to realise that the only thing she and Lucy have in common is some long-distant shared past. 'Do you keep in touch with anyone else from college?' she asks.

'Fiona, you remember her, with the blonde dreadlocks?'

Isabel nods.

'She looks very different now. She works at the hospital. Perhaps you'll meet up with her there. Tell me about the job, Iz. When do you start?'

Isabel talks about her new career, the training she undertook, the importance for her of being financially independent, her wanting to do something that benefits others. When she has finished she sees that Lucy is studying her closely.

'You're over all that stuff that happened here before?' Lucy asks. 'There was that handsome young guy. Wasn't there an accident or something? I seem to remember things were pretty heavy.'

'That was a very, very long time ago.'

'But when you come back you must think of it. Doesn't it open a whole can of worms?'

Isabel looks out of the window at the little patch of garden, at some sort of ornamental tree covered in red berries, and at the houses in the terrace behind, all their windows reflecting the sunlight. She really doesn't want to talk to Lucy any more.

She stands and picks her bag off the back of the chair. 'Thanks for the tea,' she says. She walks towards the door, comes back to give Lucy a polite kiss on the cheek. 'I'll phone,' she says. 'I've got to go now. Houses to see. I've got another house to look at. I'm sorry.' She sets off again, stops for a moment. She is flustered, not quite sure of what she is doing, surprised by her own reaction to Lucy's questions. She stands in the middle of the room and her mind goes blank. Then she comes to; things are clear again.

'I'm starting afresh,' she says. 'I don't do memory.'

Four

Daniel looks through the window of a cafe called Primary Colours. It's all black and white inside, very funny, ha ha. But it feels right, it fits his mood. The city was beautiful this morning, is dull this afternoon. Was multicoloured once. Is monochrome now. The sun still shines but the buzz has gone.

On the first day they had walked from the Gallery up this street, past the expensive shops and cafes, and somehow, he's not sure quite how, they had come to a hilltop park. Michael led the way. The grey-haired landscape painters, man and wife, followed behind carrying drawing boards and big sketchbooks in plastic bags. Isabel was deep in conversation with the black-leather philosopher poet. The man who filmed legs talked to a man who believed that underlying geology determined people's personalities. The ley-line woman sang to herself as she walked. Who else? Perhaps that was everyone. Daniel was at the back feeling, as he often did in group situations, like an outsider.

Daniel crosses the road, carries on up the hill, smiles to himself as he remembers the group of people he had chosen to be with. Isabel had referred to them as *the company of implausables*. He takes a left at the top of the hill and finds himself in a square. Grand houses built of limestone. Iron railings around a patch of grass and trees. A sign saying *residents only*. There should be an alleyway leading to the park but it has gone. There is a gap between the buildings occupied by posh cars standing on gravel. A stone wall beyond. Daniel walks through the cars, climbs the wall, drops down into the park.

He doesn't recognise anything at first. Then he walks to the top of the hill and there is the bandstand, looking just as it did before; of course it does. He sits on a park bench facing away from it and looks out at a view of the city. He remembers Michael stopping them here to say a few words: 'We'll stay two hours and meet back here at twelve-ish. Everybody to do their own thing. OK, so it's a man-made landscape. It's contrived to have an effect on our state of mind.'

There is something of the guru about Michael; a warmth and a strength of personality that makes people inclined to listen to him and believe what he says. He speaks quietly and they crowd in close to catch his words.

'Like I said last night it's the mindstuff we're after. Nothing too representational and be as spontaneous as you like. Draw what you feel. Write what you feel. It doesn't matter too much. It's just a starting point for other work – for collaboration maybe. Any questions?'

The philosopher poet takes off his sunglasses. He is a big man, heavily built, dressed completely in black – jeans, T-shirt, long leather coat. He has an amiable manner, a smile that is friendly and ironic at the same time, as if he doesn't take himself too seriously. 'This isn't the city,' he says.

Michael smiles and thinks for a moment. 'Maybe you're right,' he says. 'I think I know what you mean. But this isn't exactly wilderness – it's constructed landscape. It's an aspect

31

of the city. We'll do other stuff as the week progresses – vandalised playgrounds, post-industrial dereliction, shopping malls, multi-storey car parks, any amount of hardcore, inner-city grimness. Is that OK, Phil?'

'It's OK but I'd like more randomness. A bit of crazyness. You know, something a bit more subversive than a walk in the park. Can we do some chaos?'

'Chaos and weirdness later. I promise,' Michael says. 'This morning just the feel of this place. The contrived effect on our psychology.'

Michael pauses and looks round at everyone, leaving a space for more to be said.

'It's deeper than your psychological stuff,' the ley-line woman says. 'It isn't what people make of the land. It's what the land makes of people.' She wears an expression of wide-eyed credulity. 'There are spiritual forces in a place like this. I can feel it, honestly.'

Michael nods and tries to look interested.

Daniel finds himself speaking: 'I was stung by a bee in a place like this, a park with a bandstand. It was when I was a child. I always think of it, you know...' He becomes aware of himself and laughs out loud.

Michael waits for more but nothing comes. 'So we all bring our own stuff with us,' he says. 'That's good. It's going to be an interesting week.'

Daniel sits with his back to the bandstand, looking out at nothing. He is thinking about the hi-vis dayglow tree. It was at this time of year, a day like this one, blue sky and clear autumn light. It might look the same. He gets up and sets off in search of the tree. He takes a path between evergreen shrubs, comes to a war memorial, takes a right and walks along a terrace with stone balustrades, passes an arbour clad in hop vines, follows more winding paths. He wanders around to the back of the hill where there is more space, just grass and open-grown trees.

Everyone had spread out and started on their own work. Daniel had come across a big cherry tree, bright with autumn colour. He made a pencil sketch from the outside, as it were, from a little distance away. Then he climbed it, sat in the branches, and drew it from the inside, the patterns of sunlight coming through the leaves.

Isabel is waiting for him when he comes down. At this time she has short hair, is thin and healthy, tanned from an out-door life, wears a T-shirt and multicoloured trousers. Right now she looks serious.

'I didn't follow you,' she says. 'I'm just in the same place.'

He has been absorbed in his artwork but part of him was aware of her presence close by. He finds that these days he is always aware of her presence. He looks down at his feet. He says nothing.

She tears a page from her notebook and passes it to him. 'It's a crap poem and it's not about a tree. You may as well have it.' She turns her back to him.

He reads it through. *The hi-vis dayglow tree, and you...* He reads the whole thing a second time and she keeps her back turned all the while.

He doesn't know what to say. She is a friend, they do stuff together, that's all. She has a boyfriend called Max and the two of them more or less live together. They are talking about buying a house. She has talked about having a child with him.

Daniel likes looking at things, likes places, was good at art in school, agreed to come with her on this five-day art project even though it sounded pretentious, *Psychogeography for Beginners* – what the fuck is that about? Now he is standing under a tree holding onto a piece of paper with something written on it that sounds like some sort of declaration. He doesn't understand and he understands perfectly. She has her back to him as if she's looking at the view and her back says *here I am, there you are, you are standing quite close to me – what are you going to do next?*

'Izzy,' he says.

'I'm stupid,' she says. 'I just wanted you to read it.'

The hi-vis dayglow tree. Daniel can remember some of it now, years later. *Leaves yelloworange*, something, something, something. The tree was a neon sign, a hyperbole, something life-affirming. *Your look-at-me face, big child among the branches*, that was him then, he probably was like that. *You are very much alive*, and then on the next line, *In me.*

'It's good. I like it,' he says.

She turns to him and shrugs.

He tears two pages from his sketchbook, the drawings of the tree from the inside, and gives them to her.

'Best I can do,' he says.

Daniel is now a landscape gardener by profession and he knows about these things, about trees exhausting the soil on which they grow and settling into a period of senescence, sometimes retrenchment. All the same, he is surprised by what he finds. It is a smaller, duller tree. The leaves are sparse, limp, a dull yellow. He walks around it and then he walks away. He feels that there are times in life when, for one reason or another, you are living intensely, in full colour. The rest is monochrome. And the knowledge that he has now of the difference between the one thing and the other, between what is and what might be, that knowledge is uncomfortable. He heard somewhere, perhaps it was on the radio, that the recipe for happiness is good health and a poor memory. He would very much like to have a poor memory.

Five

In the afternoon the sun is still shining but Michael is indoors, in his studio flat near the Folly. He is not feeling a hundred per cent – that's how he would describe it if anyone were to ask. He is unsteady on his feet. His left arm doesn't work properly. His hands hurt.

He lies on his back on the bed and remembers. He was pacing, limping but pacing, the hospital corridors. He had been in for five days, didn't feel that ill, was bored, walked up and down. He couldn't go out as he had to hang around in case the machine became free and he could have his scan done. Near the end of the corridor a man was sitting on the floor pulling a dressing gown around himself with one hand and holding a mobile phone to his ear with the other. Michael tried not to look but didn't succeed; the man had a scar all the way across his neck, the flesh held together with metal clips. It looked like his head had been taken off and put on again, rather badly, perhaps by someone who hadn't done that sort of thing before. As Michael drew near the man spoke into the phone and Michael couldn't help but overhear. Understatement, the British have made it into an art form. The man held the phone to his ear and with the other hand he now wiped away the tears that were running down his cheeks. He spoke the following words: 'I'm not feeling a hundred per cent.'

And Michael, today, is not feeling a hundred per cent. The stiffness and pain in his hands have increased. He can paint but it hurts. And he knows this will get worse and then go on getting worse. He will not be able to do the few things that he is able to do now. He tries not to think about it. His hands hurt. He thinks about it. He is not feeling a hundred per cent.

He was going to do some painting this afternoon but he has taken to lying on his bed. That won't do either. He is angry and the best thing to do is to go out walking again. There is nothing quite like a brisk limp to dispel anger.

He doesn't walk far. He is on the main road that leads down to the town centre when the number twelve bus comes to a halt at the stop next to him. The door opens and two people get off. Michael gets on, pays the standard inner-city fare, finds himself a seat. He didn't intend to do this and he doesn't know where he will get off. No matter.

The bus takes him down the wide, tree-lined but busy Bedford Road. It goes around the hectic one-way system by the railway station and along Canal Street. When it crosses the water he looks to see if the tide is up but it isn't. The bus goes past two blocks of council flats and over the hill to St Peter's. Along by the docks, through Tompkin's Square and up Doubleday Street. There are two cafes here: Primary Colours and The Ferry, the first one too pretentious, the second one a bit twee. Michael stays on the bus. Past the university buildings, around two sides of the Triangle. OK, he has made up his mind. He gets off by the old graveyard and walks to the Corner Cafe.

He goes in, buys a coffee, limps across the room to a

window seat and spills half of it in the saucer. A man is watching him from a table at the side. He has a narrow face, dark hair, that's as much as Michael can take in as he passes; he is fed up with the *do-I-know-him?* thing and looks away, out of the window. He is aware that the man has got up and gone to the counter. Then he arrives at Michael's table with two cups. He puts one of them down in front of Michael and grins.

'Got you a fresh coffee,' he says. 'This one's more in the cup and less in the saucer.'

'Thanks,' Michael says.

'It's a pleasure, Mike. Long time no see.'

'Tony!' Michael says, smiling. 'Honestly I didn't recognise you at all – not until I heard your voice. How's things?'

'Well, I'm outside not inside, that's good. I'm not working but I'm looking, keeping my head down. I'm at Lynne's place, my daughter. Did you ever meet her?'

Michael shakes his head.

'You alright?' Tony asks.

'Yes, I suppose so.'

'Limping bad.'

Tony is a nice man, gentle and warm-hearted. He was one of a group of inmates at Her Majesty's Prison, Riverside, that Michael taught for a while. Michael is genuinely pleased to see him.

'I've got Parkinson's Disease,' he says.

'Fuck me. That's serious, isn't it?'

'It's not too bad. No, it's bad enough and it gets worse. But... well, I still do lots of things.'

'Lots of art?'

Michael nods.

'Teaching at Riverside?'

'No, not now.'

Tony's voice is full of concern. 'I'm very sorry to hear you're ill. You were good fun, Mike. More than that, you were an inspiration. There were some people in that group – there were twenty-something of us at one time, wasn't there? – there were some people that it helped. It's true. I mean really helped, more than just passing a couple of hours away.'

'Thanks.'

Michael sips his coffee and tries to remember when he last saw Tony. He thinks Tony looks just the same, not older certainly, perhaps a little skinnier, but then he was always slim. 'What's it like being out?' he asks.

'Scary. Scary at first. You miss the routine. And the blokes, not all of them but I was lucky, there were some good guys on my wing. So I get lonely a bit. And then I have bad dreams of being inside again.'

'But it must be good to be out in the world.'

'Yeah, of course it is. Don't get me wrong, Mike, sometimes it's fucking marvellous – excuse my French. But then you can get funny with it, bitter about what happened. I did two years, you know. It makes you go a bit crazy. I can tell it to you, I don't tell everyone.'

'I bet you don't do any art work.'

'No. People would know I've gone daft then, wouldn't they? Perhaps I should. But no, it's not really in me to get myself to do that stuff. Sorry.'

'It's alright.'

There is a silence while Tony rolls a cigarette. Michael feels uncomfortable. He knows that he has been asking Tony the right questions and listening to what he says. But he feels a lack of sympathy. This man – a good man, Michael has nothing against him – this man can put all the bad stuff behind him and can have so much ahead. So much future. That is something Michael feels he doesn't have. So how can he sympathise with people's ordinary difficulties or even their bigger problems? They all have something Michael doesn't have and he is envious of that. He thinks it hardens him a bit. And that's a loss too. He hopes that Tony is not aware of a coolness on his part.

'Do you remember big Tom?' Tony asks.

Michael nods and smiles. 'Oh, yes.'

'You'll never guess what he's up to now.'

And Tony fills him in on some of the latest gossip about different people they remember from those days. Michael gets to hear some stories that couldn't be told out loud in that place. More coffee. Chocolate cake – Tony insists on that. Lowered voices when they talk about unsavoury topics. Laughter.

Eventually they leave the cafe together although they will be going in different directions. Tony lights his cigarette as soon as he is out of the door. 'Take care, mate,' he says, and sets off down the street. Then he stops and turns back. 'Mike,' he says. He takes a pen out of one pocket, scrabbles about in the others for a piece of paper and finds an old train ticket. He writes something on it.

'It's my phone number. If you need anything, like. I don't know what but if you need a hand or something...'

Michael takes the ticket. 'Thanks. I really appreciate it.' He smiles, there's a moment's eye contact and then they both turn away before they get embarrassed.

'See you, then,' Tony says as he walks off.

Michael takes a short cut through the graveyard and then

turns down Petty Street. He will walk all the way home now; most of it is downhill. Then he will have a bath. Maybe start a new painting.

Some people don't know what to say when they hear about his illness. Others, like Tony, are just straightforwardly sympathetic. It's a funny thing, a good thing, this sympathy. Michael decides to forget about being envious of other people. They are kind, most people are kind. It's a warm thought.

Petty Street runs down a long gentle slope and he walks without a limp at all. He sees that many of the terraced houses are now painted in bright, sometimes gaudy, colours – that's good. He sees potted geraniums flowering on doorsteps and a cat sunbathing in a window. He passes a teenage boy polishing a motor scooter and a distinguished-looking, middle-aged man poking about in a skip. A bicycle has found its way into the lower branches of a tree. Fliers for a rock gig are pasted to the telegraph poles. He likes this. There is something worthwhile about it all.

Six

It is two o'clock in the afternoon and Isabel stands on a bridge that crosses a narrow reach of the harbour. She is tired of driving through heavy traffic and searching for places to park and has abandoned her car for a while. She has swapped her expensive leather shoes for an old pair of trainers, better for walking the city streets. And she is thinking about buying a flat rather than a house; a flat in the elevated part of town, walking distance from the hospital.

The bridge connects two different parts of the city: on one side are warehouses and small industrial units; on the other there are some of the oldest timber-framed houses and some of the newest glass and steel office blocks. A small park runs alongside the water, busy with late-lunching office workers and parents with young children. It looks like a safe, friendly place to sit down for a while. Isabel leaves the bridge and goes to the nearest bakery, makes her way to the park carrying a sandwich and a polystyrene cup of tea. She finds a bench on which to sit and eat her lunch. The sunshine is warm on her face and she relaxes, daydreams, becomes altogether less business-like. A man passes by on a bicycle.

She has an automatic response to even the slightest hint of certain uncomfortable memories; a mental barrier comes down and she simply thinks of something else. She has good reasons. But now she remembers a nonsense word from a long way back, *woowoowoo*. It makes her smile. And maybe it is alright to think of this: day two, Dan, Phil and herself on bicycles, a random journey. It was fun. Like a little holiday.

They cycle along the edge of the harbour, weaving from side to side, taking care not to get their wheels stuck in the railway lines that are set into the concrete. Phil leads the way on a bicycle too small for him, his knees sticking out sideways, his long coat flapping over the back wheel. Isabel follows him and behind her rides Daniel; she keeps looking over her shoulder to check that he is still there. They stop often enough but there is a sensation of constant movement. It is a sunshine and showers day; great blasts of light coming though gaps in the clouds, darker moments when the air is freshened by rain.

'Hello puddles,' Isabel calls out. 'Hello buildings, hello cranes, hello dog-and-toddler woman with pushchair.' Her face hurts with too much smiling.

'What's she on?' Phil asks, swerving to avoid a coil of rope.

'I can't imagine,' Daniel says, grinning. He follows their tyre tracks from puddle to puddle.

They come across a large number of iron bollards, up-rooted from their original places and dumped here on the dockside in groups of two or three, leaning against each other like drunken revellers at the end of a party. They get off their bicycles and wander around, looking at them.

'Better than art,' Daniel says, but he gets his sketchbook out and begins drawing them.

'What is the collective noun for bollards?' Isabel asks. She is trying to look serious but finds that it is not possible.

'A convention,' Phil says. 'Or maybe a hub-bub. A hub-bub of bollards.'

'Fuck art, let's dance,' Daniel says. He turns a page over and starts a new drawing.

'Fuck dance, let's art,' Phil says. He has taken a spray can from his bag and is making a sad face on one of the bollards.

'Leave them alone,' Isabel says. 'You're robbing them of their dignity.' She walks among them and admires their handsome shapes and the shadows they cast on the concrete. She sees that Daniel is facing out across the water, looking into the distance.

'It's going to rain,' he says.

They stand together and watch the sky darkening in the south-west, a big bank of cloud rolling in. Soon the buildings on the skyline are obscured by a greyness that spreads towards them across the city. They feel the wind pick up and hear the hissing of raindrops on water. They pick up their bicycles and move into the open doorway of a warehouse, standing just far enough inside to avoid getting wet.

Isabel watches the rain and senses Daniel standing beside her. The concrete in front of them is speckled and then uniformly darkened by the raindrops. Water collects in shallow depressions, makes puddles, flows, forms a continuous sheet marked with splashes. Then the rain ceases abruptly. Starts again. Stops altogether.

She carries on standing and watching and Daniel stays beside her. They see a belt of blue sky widening towards them and then sunlight touching rooftops. The wind has dropped. Eventually the sun reaches them and the concrete begins to steam.

Phil arrives from somewhere. 'Show over,' he says, and

pedals away. They stand silent for a while longer then get on their bicycles and follow him.

A little later on they turn away from the harbour and into a street of cobbles. 'Ahahah,' Phil sings out, letting the vibrations make a random song. 'Ahahah,' sings Daniel, a fifth above. 'Ahahah,' sings Isabel, on the octave. Two old ladies watch them from a doorstep, one with a benign smile, the other one scowling, like the weather report: sunshine and showers. They cycle through a leafy square, saluting a statue of Neptune as they pass. Another cobbled street and they come out by the water again, close to the bridge. They bump up and down curbs and head into a park. They leave the tarmac path and take to the grass to avoid running into pedestrians.

'Stop, everyone,' Isabel calls out. She puts one foot down and slides to a halt. 'Hi, Lucy. How are you doing?' she asks.

A young, healthy Lucy looks amazed to see her old friend in the city. She doesn't manage to speak. She looks at the two men who have stopped a little way in front of Isabel.

'This is Phil, the philosopher,' Isabel introduces him first. She turns to him. 'Is that your real name?'

'I'm afraid it is.'

'And Dan the man,' Isabel continues, lowering her voice. 'He's with me.'

'What are you doing?' Lucy asks. 'You look like you're having fun.'

Isabel watches the two men ride off a little way and cycle up and down on the grass. 'We're doing psychogeography for beginners,' she says. 'We've taken magic mushrooms and borrowed bikes from the art centre. We're on a *dérive*.'

'I see. And where are you off to?'

'That's the whole point of it – we don't know. We're exploring. And we've got to go.' She gets herself up onto the saddle of her bicycle but doesn't move away. 'You look fantastic, Lu,' she says. 'Vibrant. Radiant. Are you in love?'

Lucy smiles and looks smug. 'Something like that.'

Isabel hitches her pedal up with one foot, ready to push off. She looks down at the ground for a moment and then back at her friend. 'Me too,' she says, and cycles away.

Isabel walks through the park, past the ruined church and the children's playground, taking the direction she took that day. She remembers riding over a suspension bridge, a narrow elegant structure just wide enough for a bicycle, crossing a big road – four lanes, maybe six lanes of traffic hurtling underneath them. And then they rode straight into a multi-storey car park. A lift door opened, a man in a suit stepped out, they cycled straight in – one, two, three of them squeezed in together.

'Going up,' Daniel says, pressing the button for the twelfth floor.

And out on top they ride around among the cars, look out across the city, stop by the parapet and look down on the people below. The exit road is a downward spiral, a helter-skelter for cars. Or bicycles, perhaps. They career right down to the bottom and then get the lift up to the top again.

They get off their bikes and walk around looking at the view. The sun comes out from behind big clouds and they stand and admire the city.

'Woowoowoo,' Phil says, in a tone of appreciation.

'What?' asks Daniel.

'Woo*woo*woo. Emphasis on the second syllable. It's an

46

African word, Swahili or something. It means *nice arse*.'

'Whose arse are we talking about here?' asks Isabel.

'The world's arse,' Phil says. 'I'm using the word in its metaphorical sense. Something very wonderful, extraordinary or suchlike and it's woowoowoo. Or, in plain English, *get a load of that*. It's a new word just waiting to be added to the language.'

'Woowoowoo,' Isabel says, looking out across the city.

Later on they take a much graffitied and broken-glassed underpass below the motorway and find themselves in a scruffier part of town. It's a mixed area of West Indians, a few Asians, old white hippies and punks. Not a business suit in sight. Phil stops them outside a red-brick pub called The Plough. They padlock their bicycles to a lamp post and go in, Phil leading the way.

Inside it is gloomy and their eyes take time to adjust. They can see Victorian brass fittings and big mirrors, a group of elderly Jamaican men sitting around a game of dominoes. There is silence, then one of the men slams a domino down onto the table. Isabel jumps at the sound. Silence again. They become aware of the publican, a sturdy black man in his late forties, a touch of grey in his hair and beard, giving them a stern look from behind the bar.

'Have you come to play dominoes?' he asks, his voice loud in the stillness. 'This pub is only for people who play dominoes. You hear what I'm saying?'

'We could learn,' Phil says, brightly.

More silence. Then the publican slaps his hands down against the bar and bursts out laughing. He picks up a cloth and wipes the bar top, still laughing to himself. The domino players, smiling and chuckling, carry on with their game.

The man looks up and motions for the three of them to come over. 'I'm just kidding you,' he says. 'I do it sometimes to strangers coming in, I can't resist it, the look on people's faces.' He smiles at them. 'The truth is everybody is very welcome here. That's the real truth. What are you having?'

Daniel stays at the bar for a while talking to the man. Isabel sits with Phil and half-listens to his talk of surrealist automatism, the Situationists, urban ambience, psychic atmospheres. Mostly she watches Daniel. He and the barman are joking about something at first but then they are talking seriously, nodding their heads in agreement. If she was here with Max, she thinks, it would be difficult. There would be some middle-class liberal angst thing, some inverted racism that's maybe not inverted at all. And some macho posturing, a little hint of bravado about Max's manner that would put people's backs up. Daniel is different: here is the man behind the bar, let's talk to him. Or don't talk to him, no problem.

She hasn't eaten for a while. She is all mushroomed out; just beginning to come down. She has drunk half of her pint of beer very fast. Do these things explain what is going on with her? No. Is it because Daniel is attractive, sexually attractive to her, nice arse is the least of it? No, it's much more than that. Is it his wide-eyed insouciance, the straightforwardness of his manner? No. Is it the way he looks at her, sometimes he takes her so seriously? No, these things do not account for the way she feels now, not entirely. Phil is talking about the *Introduction to the Critique of Urban Geography*, the words come through to her clearly, but she has no idea what they are meant to convey. Daniel is beautiful to her, that's what it is. She knows this. She knows what it means.

He comes across from the bar with more beer and packets of crisps.

'What were you talking about?' asks Isabel.

'Psychogeography.'

'No,' she says.

'OK, so we didn't use that word. But we were talking about places, people's connection to places. He and his wife are saving up to go back to St Lucia and buy a piece of land. They want to run a smallholding. *To put something of themselves into the place*, that's what he said. And I talked about some of the work I've done outdoors. About how it's a two-way thing – the place where you work impacts on you and you leave your mark there as well, and it means something, it's worthwhile. He said I should come and visit them on the island.'

'Wow.'

'And it's so simple. All this stuff that Michael talks about, the precise laws and effects of geographical whatever-it-is, he keeps on about it. I mean, he's a good guy, I like Michael, he's really alright and he sounds inspiring until you think about it a bit. But I've worked on the land, not much but some. And it's realer than all this theoretical arty stuff. It is. And then there's you, Phil,' Daniel says, turning to him and smiling. 'You're a very nice man too. I like you, I really do. But sometimes you do talk a load of old bollocks.'

The two men grin at each other. Phil shrugs. He lifts his pint and drinks. 'Cheers,' he says, clinking his glass against Daniel's. They drink together and then laugh out loud.

Isabel looks on and wonders. The three of them fall into silence, perhaps they are all coming down off the mushroom trip. Eventually Daniel catches her eye and smiles. He touches his glass against hers. They carry on looking at each other for a while but they don't say anything.

Isabel remembers all of this very clearly. She walks on underneath a group of small trees, some of their yellow leaves have already fallen to the ground. The path turns and slopes down to a footbridge. Is this it? Only an insipid utilitarian structure passing over an ordinary side street? She walks across to the multi-storey car park. In front of her are a pair of grey swing doors with the words *Level Two* stencilled on them in black paint. She pushes through. To one side, not straight ahead as she expected, is the lift, with a sign attached to the door saying *Out of Order*. She stands looking at it for long enough to notice the smell of piss hanging in the air. She goes back through the swing doors and finds that there is a continuation of the path to one side of the car park. Perhaps there are two bridges, this one and a bigger one further on. The concrete path carries on between brick walls, curves around the side of a building, and comes to an end at a steel grill. She can't go any further. She turns around and goes back the way she came.

Seven

Deep crap. Daniel opens his eyes at the beginning of the second day of his return to the city, realises where he is, thinks *deep crap.* When he first saw the house his spirits fell; such an ugly, dirty, mean-looking little end-of-terrace hovel, squashed between a railway embankment (which blocks out the light to the rear windows) and a busy rat-run of a road. He had already said yes, he would stay here for a few days, feed the cat, enjoy a taste of city life; he was stuck with that decision.

He now knows that the inside of the house is also deeply unpleasant. A little dirt never did any harm, Daniel isn't a particularly clean and tidy person, never has been. But that grey sofa in the living room: two parts ingrained dirt to one part worn-down worn-out piece of furniture. And the bucketful, yes, bucketful of cigarette ends by the fireplace. The bare light bulbs and the grubby walls. The mould in the kitchen. The reeking toilet. And the room he wakes to find himself in, the spare room: a narrow bed with a soggy mattress; a window that would look out onto the railway embankment but one pain is grimy enough to be opaque and the other is broken and held together with Sellotape and a piece of cardboard; and an implausibly thick coating of dust on everything, layer upon layer, dust that must have been collecting since the dawn of geological time. This is why he must be out and about all day, exploring the city and staying away from the house on, wait for it, Paradise Road.

Where will he go today? He has a bizarre mental map of the city, mostly blank but marked with a few places that he remembers and doesn't want to revisit. He gets out of bed, pulls on some clothes and thinks of the place he didn't go to, the thing Michael kept talking about, the special trip that was planned for the last day, away downstream and out of the city to where the river widens out and there on the bank stands a lighthouse. The Little Red Lighthouse. Michael mentioned it often, called it *Little Red*, and told them that they would be surprised when they saw it. Today Daniel will go there.

He is soon out of the house and walking away from Paradise. He passes through a visually unappealing neighbourhood of small industrial units, warehouses and vacant lots. There is a car respray workshop with a multicoloured Alsatian dog chained up outside. There is a pub called the *PLE REE*; some letters are missing from the sign but there are adverts for cider and a flaking mural of a tree on the wall so Daniel can guess its full name. And there is a heavily fortified stone-mason's yard with a selection of gravestones visible through the chain-link fence. He hurries past.

He walks through a shopping precinct and down a busy street until he comes to a canal. He walks alongside it for some distance, eventually crossing over on a footbridge and continuing along a weedy towpath. He comes to the busy road system by the swing bridge and thinks again, against his will, of the words *you're a good friend, I'm glad you're here*. Was it on the first afternoon? He thinks it was; Michael had brought them there to see the tide coming in – he had a bit of a thing about tides.

Daniel heads on past allotments and into the gorge. He is on what might once have been a railway track, he can't be sure. The path goes through a thick growth of young trees, most of them still green, some turning a little yellow or brown. When there is a gap in the vegetation he can see the smooth surface of the river (the tide is coming up now), the fast road on the other side, and the limestone cliffs of the gorge behind that.

After walking for half an hour without meeting anyone he comes to a place where the track runs close to the water. A man a little younger than himself sits smoking and fishing.

'Hello,' Daniel says.

'Morning.' The man gives him an unfriendly look.

'Can you tell me how far it is to the Little Red Lighthouse?'

'Never heard of it.'

Daniel is perplexed. 'Are you sure?' he asks.

There is a moment's silence as the man looks him over. 'Are you taking the piss?' he asks.

Daniel feels he should leave it. 'No problem,' he says.

He walks a little further, hears the ringing of a bicycle bell behind him and steps out of the way. On the bicycle is a man and a toddler of uncertain gender strapped to a seat on the back. The child turns to look at Daniel as they go past. Daniel is in a strange place and a strange mental state, far away from his usual circumstances. He is surprised to find himself thinking of home, of his present girlfriend, Sarah, and her little girl, Elly. He hopes that they are OK. He feels a sense of responsibility for them and for their happiness. This is something new for him; he is changing, growing up maybe. It feels right. And yet at the heart of that relationship there is an open space where stronger, deeper feelings might be. He knows this for certain. But he can't work out what it means.

Now he thinks about Little Red. Michael spoke of it with enthusiasm but in an ironic tone. Perhaps it was a game of his and the place was a fiction. It is a dull grey day and Daniel is making a long journey on foot to somewhere that doesn't exist. He has these lost-the-plot moments in his life sometimes. It doesn't matter, the journey, even today's journey, is worth it anyway; he has always felt that. But what must it be like for people who don't enjoy the journey? He knows such people exist. What happens to them when they realise that there is no point to their lives other than life itself. It must be hard.

He goes on. And on. The slopes on either side of the river get less steep and the land flattens out. The river itself gets wider. Two hours pass, the tide has now turned and he comes to the edge of a small town or suburb. He passes through a council estate, stopping three times to ask people about the lighthouse. No one has heard of it. He comes to an ordinary town centre, goes into a baker's shop and buys something to eat. He walks around asking about Little Red. He thinks he should be making a list of the replies he gets:

'You're pulling my plonker, aren't you, mate?'

'Are you taking the piss?'

'Follow the yellow brick road and turn left at never-never land.'

Perhaps that was what Michael was after five years ago; it was one of his psychogeographical experiments.

Daniel asks a couple of old men sitting on a bench by a patch of grass.

'Never heard of it,' one of them says.

'The Little Red Lighthouse?' the other one says. 'Why do you want to go to the Little Red Lighthouse?'

'I don't know.'

'It does exist. I think it's still there. You go down the High Street and past the church, take the first right opposite the school...'

Daniel listens carefully and follows the directions. He finds himself walking down a track across a flat landscape of urban-fringe farmland. The fields are overgrown with brambles or grazed by ponies and goats. There are more abandoned fridges and supermarket trolleys than there are trees. He is aware that he is walking away from the river.

At the end of the track he comes to a fenced enclosure and a sign saying *Stanton Household Refuse Collection Centre*. Standing on the concrete are a number of large yellow skips and a wooden site hut. Behind the enclosure is a large grassy mound, the remains, he thinks, of the original tip. He goes in through the gates and a man comes across from the hut to greet him. Daniel asks what seems to be a pretty stupid question: 'Do you know where I can find the Little Red Lighthouse?'

The man is dressed in orange overalls and an ancient tweed jacket. He has amazing thick grey eyebrows. 'Follow me,' he says.

He leads Daniel across the yard and through a gap in the line of skips. The concrete gives way to an uneven surface of crushed rubble. In front of them is a family: man, woman, child and dog; all made out of scrap timber; the man and woman stand eight feet tall. To one side is a space rocket made out of bits of rabbit netting, a fireguard, rubbish bins and other scrap wire. There is a car built out of the insides of washing machines. And there is a horse composed entirely of plastic milk bottles; it stands in a glasshouse constructed from old metal-framed windows. At the back, about twelve feet tall, is a scrap timber and plywood lighthouse that was once painted red.

Daniel walks around everything to see how it has been put together. At last he goes up to the lighthouse and touches it with his hand. Mission accomplished. He goes back to where the man waits for him.

'Found what you're looking for?' the man asks.

Daniel doesn't answer.

The man looks out across the flat landscape towards the horizon. 'See that small patch of blue sky?' he points it out. 'It's coming this way. Two more hours of grey and then sunshine for the rest of the afternoon. A cold night. Showers tomorrow. From here you can see into the future.'

'It's a big sky,' Daniel says.

'Oh, aye. It's a grand place to do some thinking. Do you want a cup of tea? The kettle's just boiled.'

They walk back through the skips to the hut. Once inside, the man lights a camping stove and reboils some water, makes two cups of tea, passes one of them to Daniel.

'My name is Toby, by the way.'

'Dan.'

They shake hands.

'Little Red was the first thing I made here,' Toby says. 'I like this place, the light, the openness and so on. People come and then they go away again. It's pretty quiet. But I needed something to do so I started making things. Word got around and I started selling a few. I sell all the best ones, what you see are the ones nobody wants.' He lowers his voice as if he is going to tell a secret. 'They call them sculptures, you know.' He shakes his head.

'I like the horse very much,' Daniel says. 'Why is it in a glasshouse?'

'Because it would blow away otherwise. We get some wind here. It's a wonder it doesn't all blow. I have lost one or two.'

'Do you know a man called Michael Marantz?'

'The artist, you mean? Yes, but I haven't seen him for a while. He used to take a session at Riverside – I don't suppose you know about Riverside do you?'

'No.'

'He's a very good man, is our Michael. I hope he's alright.'

'Did he bring a group of people here once?'

'Aye, that's right, just the one time. It was some years ago.' He creases his eyes up and looks inward, trying to remember. 'A strange crew they were. Funny looking. And all very solemn. I think something had gone off with them. A woman started crying right in the middle of the yard. I said *has somebody died or something?* but they all shook their heads. He didn't bring people after that. I didn't want him to. I like my peace and quiet.'

'They shook their heads?' Daniel asks.

'What? Oh, aye, *nobody's died*, Michael said, but he seemed upset too. He didn't bring people any more after that.'

Daniel finishes his tea. 'Thank you.'

The man Toby looks at him kindly. 'I like the space here, you see,' he says.

Daniel stands up to leave. 'Thank you very much.'

Eight

Michael and his ex-wife, Christina, meet at regular intervals in an anonymous cafe in a nondescript part of town. The place is tacky: formica-topped tables, vinyl upholstery, nylon curtains. They long ago ceased being amused by the inappropriateness of its name: As You Like It. But they can speak freely here; they are unlikely to bump into anyone they know.

Today Michael comes in through the door and finds her already at the counter paying for her tea and biscuits. They exchange smiles and he joins the queue. After a while he catches up with her at the table. She looks as she always does, sturdy and handsome and capable.

'You're on time again,' she says, pleasantly. 'I'm almost getting used to it.'

'That's how I am these days,' he says. 'More considerate of other people. More thoughtful. Or am I kidding myself?'

She doesn't answer. 'How are you?' she asks.

'OK.'

'Good.'

She thinks for a moment before speaking again. 'You are more considerate, it's true. When we were together you never bothered. It still makes me cross when I think of it.' She smiles. She doesn't look cross.

'I've matured,' Michael says. 'It's been a long time.'

'No. It's because I'm an ordinary person to you now and you exercise ordinary politeness. As a wife I was something less. I was almost invisible.' She sounds matter of fact, not bitter.

'I'm sorry.'

'And you never apologised. That's changed too.' She sounds like she is enjoying herself.

'OK. I'm sorry I never said I'm sorry.' He laughs. They have had versions of this conversation many times and each time it is easier. It has gone from being an angry exchange to a cathartic ritual and now it is simply a habit. Like meeting in a cafe an inconvenient distance from either of their homes. And it reminds them that things were bad once, when they were married, but things are easier now. And that they have the same sense of humour.

'Have you heard from Zoë?' Michael asks.

'Not since I saw you last.'

'I dreamt she had come home.'

Christina doesn't respond to this. She is thoughtful for a while. 'I need to know more about your health,' she says.

'It's slow. It's downhill but it's a very slow downhill. I'm alright and I'll go on being alright for quite a while, I hope.' As he speaks he is aware that this is not the whole truth. There are days when he feels things are getting worse more quickly than he'd anticipated. It feels better not to say that.

'Are you painting?' she asks.

'Yes. I did a memory painting, blurry, like an old photo-graph. It was of two people sitting on a garden bench, turned slightly away from each other. I'm very pleased with it.'

They concentrate on their tea and biscuits for a while. Then Michael pushes his chair back and starts to pull his sweater off. He has difficulty getting his left arm out of the sleeve. She starts up to help him and then something makes her decide that he should do it on his own. And he only finds it awkward, not impossible. He can manage.

'It's hot in here,' he says. And then, in a different tone of voice, 'Sometimes it's humiliating. Yesterday I had difficulty doing up my shoelaces.'

Christina looks concerned but says nothing.

'How's work?' he asks.

'There's a new boy in my class. He comes from a very dysfunctional background and his behaviour is terrible. It's a challenge finding a balance between disciplining him and giving him encouragement. And I have to try not to ignore everybody else.'

'So it's stressful at the moment?'

'It's a challenge, a fulfilling challenge. But I'm glad I don't do it full time.'

She talks to him for a while about her school: the different pupils, the parents that she gets to meet, the members of staff, the financial difficulties. Eventually she falls silent.

'I liked teaching,' Michael says. 'The class I took at Riverside, the extramural classes. I liked that role.'

'I know you did.' She speaks sympathetically.

'I miss being that person. The person I can be now is not enough for me. Do I sound egotistical?'

'Yes. But you gave a lot.'

'Do you remember the psychogeography thing I did?'

She nods.

'I saw someone who looked like a young man who was on the project. And then on the way here I used the pedestrian crossing on East Street and a red car stopped to let me cross.

The woman driving it looked like someone from the same course.'

'It was on your mind.'

'I was sure it was her but she looked right through me.'

'There you are then.'

'Maybe.' Michael stares out at nothing. He doesn't say anything for a little while. When he speaks again it is in a quieter, lower tone of voice. 'They were in love. The most in love people you can imagine. I'm not sure how much they realised it themselves at first but everybody else could see it. They left an impression on me. You know what I thought?'

'No.'

'I thought that I had never been in a relationship like that. Never been in love like that. It made me feel a little sad. Envious, I suppose.'

'It contrasted with the relationship you were in at the time.'

'I didn't say that.'

'But you thought it.'

He is taken aback. 'I'm sorry, yes. It did affect my perceptions. I didn't understand at the time and maybe thinking about it in retrospect gives a false idea... but yes, I think it made me draw back from you.'

Now Christina is thoughtful and reflective too. 'I never knew. You never spoke of it.'

'I was busy. Things were complicated. But it did affect me.'

There is a silence as both of them think this over.

'And they walked into the sunset and lived happily ever after?' she asks.

He shakes his head and smiles. 'I don't know. There were problems – some bad stuff. But I don't know how it turned out in the end. I would like to find out because, in a way, I feel implicated. Perhaps some of it was my fault.'

'You had better tell me the whole story.'

'No, not now. Let me get it straight in my head. Perhaps I can tell you about it next time we meet.'

She looks at him carefully. 'I'm concerned about you,' she says. 'Will you phone if you need anything? I won't mind.'

He looks around the As You Like It Cafe, at the grease marks on the walls, the half-dead potted plants on the windowsill. Has it always been as bad as this? Perhaps it has. Sometimes, today for example, he can't believe how awful it is.

'There is one thing,' he says.

'Yes?'

'When we meet next, can it be somewhere other than here? I've had enough of this place.'

Michael takes the bus home. The weather is dull now, the city streets are without interest; he looks vaguely out of the window but his mind turns inward. He remembers leaving the house one morning and walking down to the Gallery to meet up with the psychogeographers. He was irritable, almost angry at the lack of warmth in his marriage. Christina never wanted to make love in the morning, the nearest thing to passion would be a prim, lips-closed kiss. It seemed to him that their relationship had run out of steam and he had had enough. They were friends really, that was all, and they were very independent of each other. He now had a studio complete with electric kettle, toaster, and an old double-bed mattress in the corner so he could crash out if he was painting late into the night. It would be perfectly acceptable, he told himself, if he were to pursue another relationship.

He arrived at the Gallery and saw the almost-lovers, Daniel

and Isabel, circling around each other, very happily on the brink of something extraordinary. Seeing them didn't make him feel sad; that was a later interpretation. No; he was on their side and they lifted his spirits. They would do some serious loving; he was sure of that. And what about himself, Michael Marantz? He thought that good things would come his way too, intense experiences, perhaps a love affair. Why not? It had made him feel happy to think that way back then. There was a lot of love in the world and some of it would come his way. If not today, then tomorrow. That is what he had believed.

When Michael gets back to his flat he starts a new painting. He makes a number of preliminary sketches, simple line drawings of a man and a woman. He wants their body language to describe their strong feelings for each other. One of the sketches is mildly erotic; it shows the woman sitting on the man's lap, her legs spread apart, her mouth against his. It's not very subtle and it's kitschy. He crumples it up and puts it in the bin. He makes some attempts to draw a couple embracing but they all look like visual clichés. He is most pleased with a drawing that shows the couple standing side by side, looking out at something, the woman's fingertips touching the man's forearm.

He turns the sketch into a memory painting. He makes a textured background, rolling paint onto a canvas and allowing it to dry. He draws on the two figures with charcoal. Then he works slowly and carefully with strips of torn paper and lines of paint until the figures are partially obscured. It looks like a memory; that's his intention. But still the two figures, the woman stretching out her arm to touch the man, retain a vividness and immediacy. As if it is happening now.

He looks across the room at his earlier painting, the one of himself and Christina sitting at a significant distance from each other, and then looks back at the newly finished one. He is aware of the vast difference between what is and what might be. It makes him feel bad. But he knows it is the insight of the moment; tomorrow he will look at the paintings and think only that they are good or not good. He might remember the minute or two of unnecessary emotion and wonder what the fuss was about.

Nine

The psychogeographers are spending some time working on collaborative projects on the top floor of the arts centre. The ley-line woman (she is called Val and has a loud voice) is arguing with the geology-affects-personality man (Doug, he sneezes a lot) about psychic forces in the landscape. Phil, the philosopher, is talking to the man who films feet (called Bob) about forming a smelling committee. The landscape painters are writing stream-of-consciousness soundscapes and recovering from hangovers (Freddie and Esther – they can really put it away). And Isabel and Daniel are meant to be drawing maps of their mushroom trip using different colours for different states of mind. This was Michael's idea; he smiled a great deal as he explained it to them. He wanted them to find out if their mental maps were synchronised and then determine why. They are having difficulty getting started.

'I shouldn't have come,' Daniel says.

'Because you don't want to do art or for other reasons?' Isabel asks.

'I like the idea of creativity. I like it very much that you write poems and stories, I think that's great. But... I don't know. I work hard all week and then I want to do nothing – not really nothing but exploring places, walking about, looking at things. I don't need to make art out of it.' He hesitates for a moment. 'I'm thinking about going travelling again.'

'No.'

'What do you mean, *no*?' He smiles at her.

'I mean... I suppose I don't want you to go away.'

He waits for more but that is all she is prepared to say.

'OK,' he says. 'I won't go.'

There is an awkward silence followed by a change of subject.

'You said Michael's trying to get you to make some videos,' Isabel says. 'Are you up for that?'

'Possibly, except that I don't like looking at the world through a lens – it takes something away. But maybe I can do something special with it. We'll see. I don't know what.'

'What's the thing you notice most about the city compared with rural life?' Isabel asks. She is trying to be helpful.

'Verticals. Man-made objects have lots of verticals but nature is more horizontal.'

'Trees?'

'Yes, even trees. They grow in woods and copses that stretch out sideways.'

'I am vertical but I would rather be horizontal.'

'Would you now?' he asks, grinning to himself.

'It's the beginning of a famous poem.'

'I'd like to be horizontal with you,' he says, quite seriously.

She doesn't say anything but takes a notebook out of her bag and writes: *I am vertical but I would rather be horizontal.*

'So, what's horizontal?' she asks.

'All the animals except us. All the fish in the sea.'

Isabel writes a few lines, crosses them out, writes some more.

The four-leg animals align themselves
To the horizontal land
The fish
To the horizontal sea
Even the trees make woods and copses
That stretch across the country.

'There's an unintentional rhyme but it's the best I can do for now,' she says.

'It's good.'

She struggles with another stanza.

All nature, land, and sea
Follow the horizon.
Man alone is upright
Unnatural, incongruous, feared.
Building terrible steeples.

'What do you think?' she asks.

'It's my stuff but it's your stuff too. I wouldn't have thought about the steeples but you're right. I've always thought they look sinister.'

'It's called collaboration. It's what we're meant to do.' She sounds excited. 'What else did you say, Dan?'

'You know,' he says, smiling again.

She won't return the smile but starts writing more. She takes her time. Crosses much of it out and rewrites.

I like to be vertical by day
Walking the city streets
But at night-time I lie down

And am at my most natural
Horizontal
With you
Being horizontal too.

Daniel reads her words and then looks up. 'I'd like to do some more collaboration. When do we get to be horizontal together?' he asks. It is a kind of joke but neither of them are smiling.

'I don't know,' she says.

'It's a wonderful poem,' he says.

'It's not wonderful.'

'Why not?'

'It's not serious enough. It's a one idea poem and it sounds jolly.'

'So to be good it should be sad?'

'The original poem is about being horizontal for all time. It's about longing for death. I'm afraid that happiness is shallow and only sadness is profound. That's just the way it is.'

'I don't believe you,' Daniel says. He looks at her very seriously. 'I think that happiness can be profound too. I'm sure about that.'

It is day two of Isabel's house-hunting trip to the big city. She woke early but stayed in bed daydreaming, thinking, remembering. Now she feels that she has been horizontal for too long, she can hear that Erik and Neil are up and about, she needs to get moving. She gets out of bed, takes a shower in the en suite bathroom, dresses carefully, goes down for breakfast.

Erik is at the kitchen table contemplating his cup of coffee. He is a handsome man in his late thirties, has short blond hair that is thinning a little on top, is clean-shaven.

'Morning, Iz,' he says. 'I've eaten but I'll keep you company. You've just missed Neil – he had to be off early to prepare for a really big presentation.'

Isabel smiles but doesn't speak. She sits down and helps herself to toast and coffee. Erik is polite enough to say nothing more until she has finished eating.

'House-hunting today?' he asks, finally.

She looks up. 'I might go to see a flat in Larchmont Road. It's deceptively small or deceptively large or something – I still can't get used to the spiel. It won't be as nice as this place.'

'I'm sorry,' Erik says. 'I can't help that. We're terribly rich.' He smiles and shrugs at the same time. 'No, really, it's a beautiful house and I never imagined we would be able to afford it. But Neil works so hard and I do my bit and we were lucky with the market and so on.'

'It's lovely. You've made it look very nice.'

Erik fiddles with his coffee cup and tries not to look smug. 'We've been lucky,' he says, quietly.

'Are you two alright?' she asks. 'We didn't get a chance to talk properly last night.'

'More than alright. Thanks. And we're very committed. It will be eight years in November – that's a personal best. And now we've bought the house together.'

'I'm pleased for you.'

'And are you seeing a beautiful young man these days, Isabel?' he asks.

'I was until recently but it wasn't at all serious. Not really a relationship.'

'Just another fuck, then?'

She colours a little and says nothing.

'See, I'm right.'

She shakes her head. 'Women aren't like that.'

'Oh, really.' He laughs. 'Well, I've no idea. But I do try to make some guesses.' He pauses as if to give some weight to his next words. 'Neil and I made a joint vow never to fuck anyone unless it's for love. Which means only each other for the foreseeable future. *Maybe forever*, we said. Those are the last words of the vow – *maybe forever*. It's romantic, isn't it?'

'That's wonderful.'

'Wonderful? It's unheard of in the circles we move in. People think we're crazy.' He looks down and fiddles with the crumbs on his plate. 'Weren't you in pretty deep a few years ago, Iz? A musician or something? You introduced us at a party and he was very charming.'

She takes a breath before replying. 'He played the oboe and he was called Max.'

'Max... I liked him.'

'He could be very charming, that's true. It wasn't enough to make it last.'

'I seem to remember him being in some big-time orchestra.'

'Yes, but he was number two and he couldn't stand that. He didn't get to play the solos. The first oboe was a woman, I don't know if that was a problem for him – I don't think so. But he was very ambitious. He would play the whole of the Mozart concerto from memory in the living room. I wasn't allowed in. If I wanted to upset him I would drop the words *playing second fiddle* into the conversation and he would go mad.'

She pauses and Erik waits for her to go on.

'I tried very hard to hurt him sometimes,' she says. 'He hurt me enough.'

'You must have loved him very much,' Erik says, quietly.

'What a strange thing to say.'

'To be so bitter and angry.'

'Do I sound like that? Yes, I suppose I do. Well, maybe I did love him but I'd certainly had more than enough by the end. And he was difficult. Scary, actually.'

Isabel stops abruptly. Why is she talking so much about an old lover at breakfast-time? She looks up at Erik. He is interested and sympathetic but he isn't going to push her for more. It's up to her if she wants to go on.

'Not violent scary,' she says, not wanting to be misunderstood. 'He was too careful about not injuring his hands. But he could make trouble. I didn't always understand how he did it. He was difficult, yes, but it was more than that. He had an unpleasant streak. If he wanted to he could really make trouble.' She falls silent.

Erik gets up and begins to clear the table.

'Let me do that,' she says.

'Stay as you are, Iz. You're the guest, remember.' He takes away the cups and the plates, fills the sink with hot water, empties coffee grounds into the compost bin. He never turns completely away from her and glances her way from time to time, ready to listen if she wants to say more.

'I'm being very lazy,' she says, but carries on sitting at the table.

Erik washes up and then turns to face her, drying his hands on a tea towel. 'You were unlucky,' he says. 'It doesn't have to be like that, it can be good, really. Not passionately in love, thinking of each other every minute of the day for years and years. But it can be very good.'

She doesn't say anything. She sits very still.

'Do you believe me?' Erik asks.

'I don't know.'

'You have to believe me,' he says. 'Then you have something to look forward to.'

Ten

Daniel is walking down a brightly lit street in the early evening of his second day in the city. He is tired, having walked to the Little Red Lighthouse and back, but he can't quite face going back to the deep crap house on Paradise Road. Not yet. He thinks of the PLE REE, the Apple Tree Pub. His temporary home on Paradise Road is on the edge of an area of urban decay; the Apple Tree is at the centre of it, the epitome of dereliction. But the last time he passed it he noticed a light on inside and the sound of voices; it is either haunted or still in use. He asked the man in the corner shop about it and was told to keep away from the place. It certainly looks grim, spooky, a little scary. Daniel, being Daniel and being bored, decides to look in on the way home this evening. He walks faster and is soon away from the shops and cafes of the city centre. He crosses the canal on an iron footbridge, walks along a trafficky road, negotiates a roundabout, passes down some dingy back streets, and arrives at the Apple Tree.

The pub looks unwelcoming, the door shut, the curtains drawn. He walks past and hears voices and laughter inside. He turns, goes back to the door, almost knocks but stops himself, pushes his way in. The pub has one bar, a time-warp place with 1950s advertisements for obsolete brands of cigarettes and sweets. But this is not a theme pub; the adverts, the leatherette furniture, the fittings have all been here for decades gathering dust and drink stains. The pub that time forgot. There is a fifties-type man in a grey raincoat at one end of the bar: bald head and comb-over, glasses; there should be a tatty briefcase at his feet. Otherwise it's middle-aged bikers in denim, black leather and heavy metal regalia. The barman is tall and thin, looks unwell. He puts down his cigarette and directs his eyes towards Daniel without looking at him.

'A beer please,' Daniel says. 'A pint of best... whatever you've got.'

There is a mild guffaw from behind him followed by a moment's silence. The barman looks through him and doesn't reply. A man at a nearby table speaks up: 'Cider pub this is, mate. Cider or nothing.'

'A pint of cider then, please.'

'Best, is it?' the barman says.

'Please.'

The voice behind him again: 'Might as well be worst. They only got one choice.'

The barman allows himself a bitter smile and picks up a glass. 'Best it is, then.'

Daniel carries his drink to a table in the corner of the room, sits down and takes in the atmosphere. Three bikers, one sitting, the other two standing, are at a table close by. They are the sort of men who were once physically powerful but have put on weight and gone to seed. But they are still big guys; muscle and fat straining against black T-shirts, bulging forearms covered in tattoos.

The jukebox is playing Nat King Cole:

When I fall in love
It will...

Daniel is aware that the words don't mean anything. He also realises quite quickly that the cider is very strong and it's making him feel morose. When the record stops he can hear what the three men are talking about.

'This is Jamie, Debbie's first, the one she had with that bloke from up north.'

'How old is he, then? He looks a cheeky little thing. I bet he gets into trouble.'

'He must be... well, that picture was taken last summer but now he's five, five and a half, I suppose.' He turns the page of the book in front of him. 'Look, here's my little beauty, Tracy's kid. Takes after her mother. I look after her on Thursdays, take her to playgroup. I got some funny looks at first, mind. But they know me now.'

Daniel drinks his cider and smiles to himself. Scary pub, heh? The man is showing his mates photographs of his grand-children. But it's not going to be a great night out. He can't think of what to say to anyone here; he can't believe he has anything in common with them. He drinks fast, buys another pint and a packet of peanuts, feels bored and lonely, thinks of other bad nights out he has had over the years. He tries not to think about one particular night but it gets to him. It occupies the number one slot as worst night out ever. Or worst night out so far, he thinks.

The afternoon is rainy and everyone is inside, on the top floor of the Gallery, all doing their own thing. Daniel, at a loose end, traces lines between significant points on the city maps that Michael left out for them. He shows Val, the landscape mystic, the perfect pentagram that he has drawn.

'So what are the places?' she asks, wide-eyed, excited. 'Churches or something? Sacred sites?'

He shows her the map. 'Public conveniences,' he says. 'Amazing isn't it?'

She is silent for just a moment and then laughs. 'OK. I get your point. Nice one, Dan.'

That's good then, she has a sense of humour. They are a good crowd here; nobody takes anything too seriously.

Michael is calling Isabel over to him for something. Daniel sees that she is looking concerned. She glances across at him, gives him a weak smile, turns away and goes out. Michael gives him a sympathetic look and Daniel is left wondering. Isabel returns in a few minutes and gathers up her notebooks and papers. He hangs around nearby.

'What?' he asks.

'Max. He's here for just one night and then he's off somewhere performing. I'm sorry. I didn't know he was coming.'

He watches her go out of the door and feels that something airborne has just come to ground.

After a while Val comes over. 'You alright?'

'The boyfriend's turned up,' he says.

'Poor you.' She looks at him thoughtfully. 'Don't do anything stupid, will you?'

Daniel says nothing.

Now they are all in the pub, a pleasant enough place. And Daniel's worst night out ever. Max is very charming, beams supercilious smiles at everyone, buys lots of drinks. Daniel keeps away and watches. He notices that Max does the

Napoleon-complex thing, the small man puffing himself out like a pigeon, and standing up as tall as possible, as if a string is attached to the top of his head pulling him towards the ceiling, stretching his whole body upwards. His voice is louder than necessary, his movements too flamboyant. There is something conceited about his manner. Daniel can see this but everyone else seems to like him.

He comes over. 'Daniel, isn't it?' he says. 'We met at that party last year, do you remember? And, of course, Isabel speaks of you often. So I feel I know you and we are friends already. What can I get you?'

'Nothing. No, I'll have a beer. Thanks. A pint of that one at the end there.'

Max, beaming, goes to the bar leaving Daniel feeling that he has been badly wrong-footed.

Then he is back. 'My pleasure,' he says, taking a seat opposite Daniel. 'Are you having a good time? I mean on the course. I thought it might all be very solemn but that chap Michael makes it sound light enough. I hope everybody gets something worthwhile out of it.'

'I hope so too.'

'You sound doubtful. Isabel thinks it will be a productive week for her. You know she takes her poetry very seriously – she has had several pieces accepted for publication over the years.'

'She didn't tell me.'

'Well... you know poetry is a personal thing. She has written love poems, poems about relationships. Do you write?'

'No.'

'No, neither do I. Music is my forte. But I'm merely a technician, an interpreter at most. Isabel is truly creative, a composer, with words I mean.' He lowers his voice. 'She has written very beautifully about sex.' He pauses. 'But not for publication, of course.' He leans back and smiles in a self-satisfied way. 'And she writes angry poems, very angry. Some of them are about me too – I can be a difficult muse. And your medium is...?'

'I don't know.'

There is an awkward silence.

'But you are here. That's the main thing. I'm sure Michael is very inspirational and you will come away a new man. What are you working on now?'

'A video. A short film.'

'Look, Isabel is watching us. She doesn't know it yet but I've booked us a room in a hotel. I'm sure she has had enough of that awful youth hostel. But I had better go over and give her my full attention. I enjoyed talking to you very much.'

Daniel watches him walk over to where Isabel sits with Freddie and Esther, the landscape painters. He cracks some sort of joke as he sits down and they all laugh. Daniel turns away. In the absence of anything else to do he drinks his beer down very quickly and then makes a start on the pint that Max bought him.

Phil comes and joins him for a while, sees how downcast he is and buys him another pint. Val stops beside him for a moment. She is very drunk and jolly.

'I'm going to the public fucking conveniences,' she says, smiling. And then, more seriously: 'Take it easy, Dan. Yeah?'

But Daniel is speechless. He is too miserable for Phil to be able to cope with and so he leaves him and goes over to the table where all the laughter is coming from.

Daniel sits alone and does a very good impression of an

unhappy man staring into a pint of beer. He mustn't look across at them, he knows this. He looks across. Max is leaning close to Isabel and whispering something in her ear. She is nodding and smiling. She seems unaware of Daniel's presence on the other side of the room.

He leaves the pub, heads for the city docks and soon finds himself walking along a cobbled street beside the water. There is no one about and he can speak his thoughts out loud: 'Bastard, bastard, bastard, fucking bastard.'

Is it the cobbles that make him walk like this or the four pints of beer on an empty stomach? Is there a breeze passing over the water, making little waves, catching the light, bending it, spilling it, mixing the colours? Or is it him, his muddled drunken mind and muddled drunken eyesight? What does it all mean? It means he is going to do something stupid. He knows this for sure.

He comes to the place where two stretches of water meet and the docks grow wider. Here is the youth hostel and here is Max's shiny new car, the BMW, parked outside. How beautiful it is catching the light like that, all polished and unscratched, the perfect gleam of chrome and glass. *Too obvious*, he thinks; *I'm really not that stupid.* He walks past on the opposite side of the street to avoid any temptation.

He goes on to the Gallery and uses the swipe card (Michael gave them one each) to get in.

'Fuck art, let's fuck,' he says out loud. Then he remembers that he was saving these words as a sort of joke. When the time was right he would say *fuck art, let's fuck* and he would be joking but he would mean it too. It would just come out in a seemingly spontaneous way and then he would allow himself a little eye contact with her and it would be a joke and it would be serious because he wanted her so much and it would not be fucking it would be loving. It would be loving.

Daniel climbs the stairs to the top floor. The lights must be connected to some sort of sensors, they come on as he goes up and switch off again a little later. He goes to the cupboard and gets the video camera he has been using, puts it in the faux-leather carry bag and goes out with it over his shoulder.

On the dockside he looks down on the water, at the little patches of light it reflects. He takes the camera out. Puts it away again. He walks down to the grey cranes that were once used for unloading ships here. He walks around the first one, goes to the second; checks that there is nobody about.

The first part of the climb is very difficult; the only hand-holds and footholds are the ends of bolts which have been almost covered up by the many layers of paint put on them over the years. But he manages to get to the first platform and then, for a while, it's easy; just big triangles of metal girders, a knee up, a foot up, a hand up, one careful movement at a time. The video camera in its bag swings around and catches between the girders and now it's not so easy. He must lower himself, lean outwards a little... Daniel finds that he is no longer drunk; the adrenaline has sorted that out. He manages to untangle the bag and move on.

The superstructure of the crane forms an elegant curve that takes him up and out over the water. At the far end he wedges himself into the narrow space between the girders and looks out at the city. It is made of light. There are moving lights, red going up the hill opposite him, white coming down. There are lights shining from the windows of buildings that are otherwise invisible to him. There are streetlights, orange in most places, white in the posh areas on top of the hill. Flood-lights are reflected off the cathedral and off the big statues in the square.

He gets the camera out and starts filming. To get some footage of the light reflecting up off the water he must wedge the camera between his body and the girder on his left-hand side. He leaves the machine running until the tape has played all the way through. Now he is tired and cold and cannot stop himself from pissing in his trousers. He is as high up as he can go and is at his lowest point. He hopes that this is his lowest point.

Eleven

This afternoon Michael is in the queue at the post office, waiting for his turn at the counter. He feels less than completely wonderful; he is unsteady on his feet and moving around among other people in a confined space is difficult for him. In his hand is a carefully wrapped parcel addressed to his daughter, Zoë. It is a book about subversive street theatre; just her sort of thing. He knows she will like it. The queue moves forward and Michael shuffles along. There is something about these small movements that is hard for him; his right foot doesn't quite lift off the floor and he nearly stumbles. And as usual the sense of impending embarrassment makes him feel shakier. He is tempted just to walk out. But if he gives way every time he encounters a difficulty he would do very little at all; that's not really an option for him.

The woman in front moves up to the counter and it will be his turn next. He feels nervous and then angry that such a simple chore should be so challenging for him. The light goes on to indicate a vacant position and he goes forward and puts his parcel on the scales.

'First class please,' he says.

'UK or overseas?' The woman behind the counter speaks to him gently, as if to an old person or a child.

'UK,' Michael says, putting on a business-like tone of voice to disguise his discomfort. He pushes forward a ten-pound note that he had taken out of his wallet well in advance. The woman passes the stamps and his change through to him. And it all feels like it's too much. He has to collect the coins together and put them in his pocket and his left hand isn't really working at all. He drops a pound coin on the floor and manages to pick it up again. But now he must stick the stamps on before handing over the parcel and he knows he can't do it. He feels confused, snatches at the stamps, crumples them up in his hand and walks out hurriedly, still carrying the parcel.

He limps down the street towards home feeling angry and sorry for himself. Today he has started but failed to complete a number of small chores and he won't attempt anything more until tomorrow. What hurts the most is the fact that he is losing the ability to give, to do something for others. He wanted to send a present to someone he loves and he couldn't do it. He feels that he has let Zoë down again.

And so it is that he finds himself remembering, more vividly than he would wish, a day when Zoë was still at school and living at home. He had bumped into her in town when he was in the company of someone that he didn't want to be seen with, his current *inamorata*, that's the word he liked to use back then – his secret girlfriend, the other woman. They had come out of a newsagent's together and nearly walked into Zoë. They weren't kissing or hand-in-hand or even arm-in-arm but he knew that there was enough in their body language to give the game away. He felt guilty and shifty. Zoë stared at them for a moment and then walked away without speaking. Nothing was ever said. He never asked his daughter what she was doing in town when she was meant to be at school.

He arrives back at his flat still holding the parcel in one hand and the crumpled-up stamps in the other. In his mind there is a feeling of guilt, a sense of betrayal, an awareness of being caught out doing something that was wrong. As if it had happened not a few years ago but today. Michael believes that he is not a bad man, merely foolish. But he would like to have been a better father. He wishes he had done more for his only child when he was still able to.

This evening Michael is walking, limping, back home after spending some time with two old friends who are now a couple, a very happy couple. He passes through the leafy streets of a well-to-do neighbourhood and replays their conversation in his head. He didn't talk about the painful non-event in the post office. He had tried, instead, to talk about his illness in an entertaining way. He spoke of the aurora borealis, the juggernaut and the alien within. He has these themes prepared so that he has something to say when people say *tell me your news*. He has been ambushed by that one before and he doesn't have news; he has symptoms.

He had always wanted to see the aurora borealis and now his dream has come true. All he has to do is shut his eyes at night (it doesn't work every night but often enough) and he has his own light show, green and yellow flashes spreading up from the bottom of his 'vision', waves of colour glowing and flowing and pulsating. It lasts for a few minutes and then, if everything else is OK, he sleeps.

The juggernaut effect is not so entertaining. When he is by a busy road in the middle of the day he expects to hear traffic noises. When he wakes in the night to hear the sound of articulated lorries in the bedroom he is less than enchanted. It is interesting but it's no fun.

And the alien within; that makes a good story. His body feels like it is being controlled by someone else. There are two manifestations of the alien. Number one: the movements that his body won't make. His left hand and arm, for instance, have the habit of not obeying commands and just simply not opening that door and not turning on that tap and not lifting that cup of tea. It could be worse; he is right-handed. Number two: the alien gets busy. When Michael is relaxing all he wants is for his limbs to stay put. They don't. Or at least one of them doesn't; his left leg makes sudden unexpected jerking movements when he sits down to read a book. Of course there are other symptoms but he doesn't want to bore people. And for his own sanity he must concentrate on the things he can still do. He is happy that he can still paint.

Michael's friends, Jenny and Liam, had very few symptoms but plenty of news. They have a new flat, made possible by their moving in together and combining their salaries. Jenny has a new job as an art therapist working with people who are mentally ill; it's challenging but she enjoys it. Liam has a new book coming out, *The Natural History of Churchyards*. He loved the research, enjoyed writing it, liaised happily with photographers and illustrators and has now received a small advance. It is a shame that he has such a bad cold. It is the change in the seasons. He hopes that it won't stick around like the one he had in the spring.

Michael has known each of them for a long time; he is fond of them both and enjoys their happiness and good news. But walking down these streets in the cold night air and hearing their words echoing about in his head he can't help but feel envious. They have youth (at least in comparison to him), they have energy, they have each other and they have a future. And one of them has a bad cold that will be gone by next week. Michael would give a lot to have an illness that would be over by next week. Or next year. Anything that was going to get better rather than worse. What a luxury that would be.

The weather has changed; there has been a strong wind and some heavy showers during the evening. That is why some of the leaves have come down and at the corner by the phone box the big oak has shed some acorns. A car passes by now, its wheels run over some of them and squashes them flat. Michael smells autumn. Pulverised acorns, damp leaves, fallen fruits, wet pavements. And with the days shortening it feels like everything is winding down. He thinks of the word *entropy*; isn't that something to do with it all coming slowly apart? The inevitable ending of all things in the universe. That's what he thinks about now. It's ridiculous; life goes on, his life goes on, productive and healthy enough for the time being. But he can't help but think about things coming to an end.

Twelve

Isabel is walking along the dockside between the youth hostel and the Gallery for another day's psychogeography. The cobbles are glistening wet from a recent shower, the air is cool, the sky is mainly cloud, some blue. But she is not particularly aware of her surroundings; she has a lot on her mind. She dreamed last night that she was holding a baby. She can't remember what it looked like or whether it was a boy or a girl but she remembers the feeling of the child in her arms and against her breast. Perhaps it was a very short dream; that is all that she can recall – that feeling. It comes to her very strongly as she walks along; as if that small person, her child, is with her in some way.

To clear her mind she tries to focus outwards on the world about her. It is, she thinks, a sporty kind of morning: two rowing crews on the water, some joggers, the occasional cyclist. There is a man in white practising tai chi in a car park. From a little distance he reminds her of an unsteady white candle flame, a calming presence. That's good; the sight of him stills her thoughts somewhat. She draws closer, eventually coming up to the steel fence that separates the cars from the dockside. She watches him for a moment and her mind slows down enough for her to appreciate that she isn't ready to talk to anyone right now.

Isabel walks around the edge of the car park and into a side street that leads away from the docks. Soon she is walking along the pavement of a long stretch of road by the canal. It is a good place for her to collect her thoughts, busy enough for her to feel at ease. When she feels calmer she will turn around and go back. The imaginary baby, her dream child, is still with her but not as such a strong presence. She can think rationally about this. She can't be pregnant; there is no baby. Her body, or maybe it is her mind, tells her something else. And her period is a little overdue – a week late, is it? She can't be sure. But she has a coil, they're meant to be pretty safe and besides that she has had very little physical contact with Max in the last few weeks. OK, then – no baby. She thinks of Max as a husband and father. No, it really can't be. Why not? Because Max is Max. And because she loves Daniel.

Isabel turns and starts back, walking fast. She wants a child. She loves Daniel. Two things, very clear and strong in her mind. She thinks about last night and can picture herself in the pub with Max, trying to make the best of it and all the time terribly aware of Daniel on the other side of the room. She had watched him slipping out of the pub without turning his head to look back. Now she needs to know where he is. During the last few days they have seldom been out of each other's sight and he has always been in her thoughts.

She arrives at the Gallery and makes her way to the top floor. The psychogeographers mill around; some of them clearly hungover. Daniel is not there. Michael and a quiet man called Doug are busy planning a tour of the city for everyone. They will be looking at the geology: conscious (the use of local building stone) and subconscious (the underlying rocks), as Doug puts it. They have maps spread out on a table and are drawing up an itinerary. Isabel hangs around for a while and then decides to go back to the youth hostel. Perhaps she will bump into Daniel on the way.

Max's car is still parked outside the hostel, a reminder of his presence in the city. Inside it is quiet; most people have gone now. She goes upstairs to the men's dormitories and looks in through the open doors. At the far end of one room a man lies sleeping. She takes her shoes off and approaches. It is Daniel, his back to her, his body moving slightly as he breathes. She sits down on the bed next to his and waits for him to stir. He is only half-covered by a white sheet and she lets her eyes wander over his suntanned back and shoulders, his neck, his messed-up hair. She smiles to herself; she very much wants to make love to him. But perhaps it is enough just to be here, watching.

After a while Daniel wakes up. He rolls over, pulls the sheet up over his chest and looks at her unhappily. 'Why are you here?' he asks.

'I was worried about you.'

'Oh, really?'

'Yes.' She can't say more than this for now.

Silence. Daniel looks away. He rubs his eyes, scratches his head, yawns, turns to her again. 'I don't understand.'

'You didn't come back last night,' she says. 'I stayed awake and you didn't come in. Where were you?'

'Does it matter to you?'

She nods her head. 'Yes.'

He seems reluctant to speak. 'I did some filming. I made a video.'

'What did you film?'

'I'll show it to you sometime.'

She doesn't know what to say but will not leave. She wants a reconciliation of some sort.

'I thought you went to a hotel with Max,' he says.

'I didn't.'

'That's good.' He thinks for a moment. He is perhaps a little happier or a little more awake. 'I have a lot of questions to ask you,' he says.

'Go ahead.'

'Why is Max's car here?'

'He got drunk and went off in a taxi. Next question.'

'Why are you going out with such a complete bastard?' he asks, quite seriously.

'Max can be awful, I know. But he has another side to him. He can be very loving, very giving.'

'Maybe I don't need to know this.'

'You asked.' She pauses and then goes on. 'He can be supportive and caring. And he was very keen on me. In love with me, I suppose.'

'He's arrogant.'

'He's insecure.'

Daniel laughs. 'He has a funny way of showing it.'

There is a long silence now. She feels that he is angry with her and wants her to go away. She doesn't go. 'I'll leave him,' she says. 'It will be difficult, he will be difficult, but I have to do it.'

'There's hope for me then?'

She nods.

'How much hope?'

'Quite a lot.'

Daniel doesn't speak. He lies on his back and looks up at

the ceiling. She can't read his thoughts.

There is a long, long silence. She wishes that they hadn't been talking about Max. He is part of her past; what matters now is her relationship with Daniel. She would like to tell him more but it's maybe the wrong time. Perhaps if she just sits here and waits, things will turn around.

'What do you think?' she asks, finally.

'Last night was shit. It was very bad watching you and him together. I wanted to die. Is that an answer?'

She nods her head.

'Will you get into bed with me?' he asks.

'No, not yet. There are things I have to sort out.' She smiles. 'I want to, of course.'

He smiles and then studies her face closely. 'I care about you, about your happiness,' he says.

Silence again for a while. And now the sound of an argument in the street outside. Two men's voices. Some swearing.

'Oh, my God. It's Max,' she says.

'Very good. That's very, very good.' Daniel turns away from her angrily.

She leans forward to touch him on the shoulder but thinks better of it. 'I've got to go,' she says.

'Yes, you've got to go.'

Isabel goes down to the front door and sees that Max is trying to stop his car being towed away. He is arguing with a lorry driver in a hi-vis jacket; the man has already connected a steel cable to the car's front axle and is preparing to winch it onto his truck. She stands and watches.

'I said I will pay the fucking fine now,' Max says. He takes his wallet out and waves it towards the man.

'Speak to him, not me,' the driver says, nodding his head in the direction of the traffic warden who is in charge of the operation.

Max goes up to him. He speaks very sharply, 'Tell him to leave my car alone.'

'I'm sorry, sir. I can't do that.'

'Why can't you do that? I'm here now and I'm willing to pay the fine. In cash, if that's what you want.'

'I've completed the paperwork, sir. The car has been abandoned in a restricted parking zone and it will be taken to the car pound – the address is here.' He passes Max a piece of paper.

Meanwhile the lorry driver has his ramps in place and has switched on the winch. Max's car is being dragged, handbrake still on, over the wet cobbles. Max rushes over to him and starts shouting. 'Switch the thing off. Switch the fucking thing off.'

The driver ignores him. Max steps over to the traffic warden. 'I will sue,' he says. 'I will get to you. You will be done for fucking criminal damage. Are you listening?'

'If you want the police to be involved, sir, I can give them a call on my radio.'

Max walks away. He is shaking with anger but he is still in control. Isabel guesses that he knows he has almost gone too far. She moves back into the doorway of the hostel hoping he won't see her. The lorry driver adjusts the position of his ramps and then winches the vehicle all the way on board. He fixes straps over each of the wheels, checks them carefully and drives off. The traffic warden walks away in the other direction.

And now Max does see Isabel. He walks towards her slowly, gathering his anger up and focusing it on her.

'Bad luck,' she says, because she must say something.

Max steps up and stands very close to her. He lowers his voice. 'I regard you as somewhat responsible for this,' he says. 'And you will find that you will be hurt. I will make you hurt.' He walks quickly away down the street and out of sight.

Isabel stands motionless outside the hostel, aware that her hands are shaking. She is frightened but she is also angry. Men and their fucking cars, she thinks. Then she understands that for Max it is about something more than a car. And she wonders if this is a good time to start crying. It's all so complicated. But she has a feeling that Max will keep away now. He has done his worst. And perhaps things are going be alright. Much more than alright, wonderful. It will all be sorted out in the next day or two.

Thirteen

'Landscape is memory,' Michael says. 'Of course it is; it's the product of time. Let me explain a bit by giving you an example. I have a studio in a house on Folly Hill. I know, you're right, the name does seem a bit too appropriate. But I needed somewhere to work and that's what was available. It's in the middle of a red-brick suburb, streets all laid out in a grid pattern, names like Sapphire Street and Onyx Avenue and so forth, no history, no connection to the place at all. But winding up the hill is what was clearly once a country lane. It doesn't go in a straight line for a second, it's a product of historical processes, wiggly farm boundaries, that sort of thing. And the Folly, you can't see it from here but you can see it from the other side of the city. It's quite a landmark. It was built by a rich man who wanted to spy on his neighbours, that's what they say. And so there's Fairfield Lane and the Folly and even Whitehouse Farm, all fossilised, all memory of times past...'

It is the morning of day three of Daniel's stay in the city. For the first two days the Folly was a mental no-go area for him. He didn't go near it, he didn't look at it from afar, and he tried not to think about it. Now he remembers one of Michael's little impromptu lectures; he more or less hears the words in his head, *landscape is memory.* Well, yes. Something like that. He would be able to see the Folly from here if he stopped, turned, and looked out across the city. He carries on walking but it's too late; he has been ambushed by memory anyway.

Daniel is in the posh part of town, walking along the pavement in front of a terrace of grand Georgian houses. On his left the ground drops away down to a road and a small private park. Over the treetops is the view of the city that he won't look at, not yet. Instead he glances through the windows on his right as he passes by. When he has had enough of opulent interiors he watches his shadow making its way across the paving slabs in front of him. He has decided, this morning, to walk up to the Sailor's Memorial on the grass above the gorge. It makes some sort of destination.

Daniel is finding it hard work, this filtering of memories, allowing some through and keeping others at bay. It's making him go a little bit crazy and it doesn't help that there is no one here to talk to. He normally enjoys being on his own, he works alone often enough, but it would be good to share his thoughts with someone. Not the Folly Hill stuff, he is really not ready to deal with that now. But to talk to someone about some of his nonsense, that would be very good. He is lonely.

Today he would like to escape the past and retreat into the present. He thinks of Sarah and the little girl, Elly, and the home that is slowly becoming his home. The relationship is more of a habit than a passion, he's clear about that, but it's what he wants now, something sane. What else is there? Perhaps he could go back today. He can take the bus, or, if he can get to the motorway by lunchtime, he can hitch. OK, that's the plan: up to the Sailor's Memorial for a last look at the city and then head for somewhere like home.

At the end of the terrace he turns right and walks uphill. There are few people about here this morning; it's mainly a residential area, a bit touristy at weekends, but quiet now on a midweek morning. The pavement is clear in front of him. His eyes follow the movement of a woman moving in the same direction as himself, about two hundred yards ahead. He quickens his step a little. She is walking fast and he doesn't seem to be getting any closer. He runs a few paces and then walks again. She reaches a corner, stands still for a moment, and then turns down a side street. He runs until he is almost at the corner, stops to get his breath back, and turns to follow, making sure that he is moving at a natural-seeming, relaxed pace. She is moving more slowly now and he is drawing closer. She stops to look in a shop window. He stops and pretends to tie his shoelace. He doesn't take his eyes off her for a single second. She moves on and he follows. She stops. He stops and watches her as she unlocks the driver's door of a small red car. She is maybe fifty yards away now and he can see her face in profile as she gets in. He hears the engine start, sees the indicator flashing, watches as the car pulls away from the curb and heads off up the street.

Daniel thinks that he must still be out of breath from running. He feels his face flushed and hot and knows he smiling a foolish smile. She was smartly dressed and her hair was different from the way he remembers. Stupid, he thinks. Stupid me. But predictable; of course he is going to see her here, imagine her to be in this city no matter how far away she really is; of course he will catch sight of someone who walks in the way she walked, turns her head in the way she turned her head. And he *is* crazy in some way, he knows it now. He will stay here for the rest of the week; go back Saturday or Sunday perhaps. He wants to be in the city for a few more days.

Daniel sits alone on the steps of the Sailor's Memorial and watches jackdaws dropping out of a big sycamore tree and gliding towards the gorge. Each one stalls when it reaches the edge, tucks its wings in, and drops down and away out of sight. He picks up a small stone and scratches a symbol on the marble step.

He remembers that it means 'What the fuck'. That's what Phil had said. Or 'My washing machine is stuck on spin'. That was Val's translation.

Or 'Spin on it'. Phil again.

'It's an upside-down question mark and a labyrinth,' Isabel says. 'It's the ultimate unknowing – we can't find out the answer because we don't even know what the question is.'

'You've been listening to Phil too long,' Daniel says.

She nods and smiles.

The four of them have come across this symbol several times this morning, sprayed in red paint onto the walls of derelict buildings, kerbstones and lamp posts. It fits in well with the profound nonsense of today's activity: a walk through the city following the route drawn by Michael on a map of a different place, another city far away. It guarantees that they will take truly random turnings and find things that they didn't expect. And it works. They have met a man coming out of a cafe wearing a large snake, a live one, around his neck like a scarf; watched a busking acrobat, complete with trampoline; discovered a man sleeping in a cardboard box labelled *This Way Up* (upside down, of course); and are now outside a leisure centre where they have been looking through the window at the Third International Convention of Jugglers.

'I always thought surrealist automatism was overrated,' Phil says.

'You did?' Val asks.

'Always,' Phil says, with a deliberately ambiguous smile. 'Surrendering to the dictates of the unconscious – it's not random enough. This is much better. You know the Situationists criticised surrealism because of its subordination to the sovereignty of choice.'

'I didn't know that,' Isabel says, smiling.

'Well I never,' Val says, in mock incredulity, her voice hitting just the right tone of irony and making everybody laugh.

'Sorry, Phil,' Daniel says. 'But I can't cope with this stuff. I still think it's a load of old bollocks. No offence intended.'

'None taken, mate.'

Daniel carries on: 'It really doesn't do anything for me. It's not why I came here...'

'Well no,' Val says. 'That's not why you're here.'

Daniel sits alone on the steps of the Sailor's Memorial, draws another upside down question mark, and wonders why he came to the city this time. To check out the past, he guesses. To rethink the present. To wonder about the future. That's OK, it's a reason for being here, for staying a little longer. Maybe these few days in the city are a time when past, present and future can, in some way, interact. A meeting place and a turning point.

There is an image in his mind of a smartly dressed woman getting into a red car. He finds himself thinking *what if?* He takes a deep breath. He believes that he is a different person now – *this time...* he thinks, and tries to stop himself right there. He lifts his head and starts to watch people coming and going. An old woman with a poodle. Two schoolgirls carrying violin cases. Then a middle-aged couple, walking slowly, holding hands. Daniel looks up at the sky and allows his mind to drift. *This time it will be different,* he thinks. *This time it will be very, very good.*

Fourteen

It is seven o'clock in the evening, the psychogeographers have returned to the top floor of the Gallery and they will soon be off to see one of the biggest tides of the year come flooding up the gorge, over the lock gates and into the old city docks, the beautifully named floating harbour. They are waiting for Val who, somebody says, has lost her ley line again. Michael stands in the doorway, watches people milling about and chatting, and wonders if he likes being Father Christmas. That is what Val had called him on the first day when he kept handing out more and more free art materials. 'I can't stay long – I've left my sleigh parked on a double yellow line,' he had said. And yes, he does like being Father Christmas. He likes the role of benign father figure, handing out compliments like presents, building up people's enthusiasm and confidence, getting them to try new things, to see things differently. *Art makes you see things differently*, that's what he says as often as he can.

Michael watches Daniel move across the room with a young man's grace. He has a certain amount of boyishness and manliness about him, Michael thinks. He can go from bravado to bashfulness, from look-at-me childlike egotism to genuine modesty and thoughtfulness. He has a sense of humour. He is wearing the same torn T-shirt he had on yesterday. He is in love.

Isabel sits in the corner of the room writing something in a notebook. Michael sees her lift her eyes from the page to watch Daniel for a while. She writes again. Glances up at Daniel. Writes. When she lifts her eyes for the third time Daniel turns towards her and winks. He knows exactly where in the room she is, knows when she is looking at him. A lover's telepathy, Michael thinks. There is a gravitational pull that keeps them in each other's orbit; they are at the centre of each other's mental map. It's some sort of psychological geography...

Michael's consciousness cranks up a level; he is in less of a dream now. Psychogeography, he thinks, is a stupid word; it was just something to bring people together to do some art, a word that would grab people's attention and would also look good on grant application forms. It would bring in the dosh. He looks at the almost-lovers and finds that the word has a new meaning. He likes that.

Isabel gets up, walks across the room, and speaks to Daniel. They move close but they don't touch. How do they do that, how do they keep their hands off each other? Michael smiles; he approves of their forthcoming passion. Of course he is envious too; he would like to be standing where Daniel stands, poised on the brink, the future rushing up to meet him.

And Michael is poised on the brink now, in a manner of speaking. He wants to look down into the gorge and has come up here, close to the Sailor's Memorial, and has climbed over the fence and down through some scrubby bushes to the very edge of the cliff. He sits on a rock that is out of sight of passers-by and he looks down. He is thinking about suicide. It is not an urgent thought; he is not ready to die just yet. But it is an idea for the future, for the time when he is unable to do anything at all and there is no point in living. Except that if he is unable to do anything then he won't be able to get himself here to bring things to an end. Unless they have installed wheelchair access by then to allow the disabled the same choices as everyone else. Equal opportunities, that's right, isn't it? Michael laughs out loud; there is nobody close enough to hear him. He thinks about the bridge that they had planned to build across the gorge here in the nineteenth century. It never happened, and when the idea was put forward again recently that was one of the arguments against it – it would become a focus for suicides, they said.

He looks down, watches the tide slowly covering the brown mud at the bottom of the gorge, and thinks of entropy. He looked up the word in the dictionary this morning and found that it did, in a scientific sort of way, have something to do with the end of all things, the winding down of the universe. And now, with autumn leaves scudding about in the wind and jackdaws dropping over the edge of the gorge into space, it feels like the right word for the time of year. But perhaps there is another meaning; the dictionary said it came from the Greek for *in turning, in transformation*. The tides drawing in and out and the seasons moving on tell him that the world still turns, everything is in a state of cyclical change. So he has a choice of meanings: endless decay or constant renewal. And this is how it is for him: he has some choices as to how he thinks about his circumstances. If only he can find a way of turning his thoughts towards something positive.

It is eight o'clock in the evening and the pyschogeographers wander around on the little lozenge-shaped piece of land that juts out into the water. On either side of them are lock gates; one set defunct, permanently closed, rubble and timber piled against them, sealing off the flow of water; the other set are disappearing below a rising tide. The water seems still, looks shiny and viscous, reflects stray light from street lamps and passing cars, creeps slowly higher.

Phil, in black leather, is a bulky dark presence, striding about and cracking morbid jokes. Val is crouching behind the brick lock-keeper's hut trying to light an unusually long cigarette. Freddie and Esther, the landscape painters, are already *well pissed* (as Esther puts it), and walk slowly along the stone quayside hand in hand. Doug, the geology man, talks to Michael and points towards the high ground on either side of the gorge. Bob, the foot-filmer, has no camera to hide behind tonight and lurks in the shadows. And Daniel is talking earnestly to Isabel. She faces away from the water, looks at the lights of the traffic passing over the swing bridge, and nods her head from time to time to answer his questions.

Now Michael raises his voice and calls out: '*Tout le monde, écoutez, s'il vous plaît.* Sorry to break up your reverie everybody but just a couple of words, some ideas from Doug, a few things I want to say, then we can take in the scene for a little while longer before going back to the Gallery and watching Dan's video, UK premier, no less. And, of course, we'll still get to the pub well before closing time.'

He pauses while people draw in a little closer. 'Doug's stuff first.' He turns to him. 'Do you want to tell them or shall I?' Doug indicates his preference by taking a step backwards.

'OK, so he's been telling me, and it's something to pass on while we're standing here. We're in the city, right? But there are all these natural forces. The rocks here...' he points towards the gorge, 'are 250 million years old, formed under a tropical sea, warm tides flowing in and out over the coral...' His words peter out. Doug steps forward and whispers in his ear. 'The past is always with us,' Michael continues. 'That sort of thing – something to think about... what?' Doug is whispering in his ear again. 'Geology is to landscape as the unconscious is to the waking mind. That's good, somebody write it down.'

Michael pauses while Isabel gets her notebook out. 'And talking of tides and natural processes,' he looks pointedly at Freddie who is standing behind Esther with his arms around her, rubbing himself against her like a cat. 'I know, I know, it's the moonlight.' He looks up at the dark sky tinged orange by street lamps. 'Or it would be if it hadn't clouded over.'

Michael lets out a big sigh. He feels that his preoccupation with the moon and tides is difficult to convey to other people. 'I'll say it as briefly as I can. Full moon at this time of year means equinoctial spring tides.'

'It's not spring,' Phil interrupts quickly.

'Spring as in spring forth, rise up in a big way. Spring tides come at the full moon which we could see if it hadn't clouded over.'

'I think it's going down a bit now,' Val says, looking out across the water. 'I liked the bit about the subconscious. What was that again?'

'Let's talk about it in the pub,' Phil says.

'We should see Dan's film first,' Michael says. 'It's a night-time thing, we should do it now. We'll go back to the Gallery for half an hour everybody, if that's alright.'

There is light coming up off the water: the patterns of small waves, convex and concave surfaces stretching and compressing, alternating, in constant motion. The lights of cars: red and white lights moving up and down, circulating; orange indicators flashing on, off. The lighted windows of invisible buildings. The floodlit stonework of a church spire. An illuminated advertising hoarding. Little of substance: mostly shapes, patterns, colours. Sometimes the camera shakes, sometimes it drifts, sometimes it is still. There is some recorded sound: water lapping against stone, the movement of the wind, traffic noise, a distant police siren. Then a regular rhythmic beat, gradually slowing. Darkness as the lights slide out of view. The rhythm continues and then stops. Silence.

Michael switches off the projector. He goes to turn on the lights but stops himself when he realises it will spoil the mood of the moment; the film has created an atmosphere in the room, a group sensibility that he feels he should respect. There is a couple of minutes silence before Phil speaks: 'Where were you, Dan?'

'At the top of the crane, the grey one down the docks a little way.'

Isabel lets out a small gasp.

Dan goes on: 'I wasn't having a good evening. What with one thing and another.'

Silence again.

'And that sound towards the end?' Phil asks.

'It was cold. I was tired. I thought I might fall off. I had to hold on with both hands to be safe.'

'To be safe – that's a good one,' Phil says.

'So I held the camera against my side, against my ribs.'

Isabel makes another incoherent noise.

Nobody else speaks for a little while; they are alone with their individual thoughts and their thoughts are of Daniel and Isabel. Eventually Phil tries to lighten the atmosphere with a joke: 'Daniel, my old mate,' he says, 'I think I have a new nickname for you. Something appropriate to the circumstances. Do you mind if I call you *heartbeat*?'

Fifteen

Isabel stands at the living-room window and looks out. The yellow leaves of a poplar tree obscure most of the view but she can see a small piece of grey sky. Day three of her stay here, mid-morning, not raining, and still she doesn't feel like going outside. Neil is at work. Erik has gone to the shops for something, will be back soon, set off for his part-time job later. She will have some coffee with him when he comes in, that is as far ahead as she is willing to imagine at the moment.

It is a large house: three storeys high, stone-fronted, part of a short terrace of better properties in an otherwise ordinary part of town. The living room is on the first floor, really two rooms knocked together. Big Georgian style windows bring in lots of light from both directions. There are original paintings and prints on the walls; there are big bookcases full of novels and poetry and art books; the floor is made of wide polished oak boards only partially covered by expensive rugs. Everything is spotless and in good taste. No wonder Isabel doesn't want to leave the house. No wonder she finds it hard to look for a place of her own.

She leaves the window, goes back to the sofa, sits and turns over the pages of an illustrated biography of Georgia O' Keeffe. Puts it down and picks up Carl Sandburg. She reads:

Let a joy keep you
Reach out your hands
And take it when it runs by

She lets her eyes drop to the bottom of the page.

Let joy kill you!
Keep away from the little deaths.

Maybe she once understood what this meant. *Reach out your hands and take it when it runs by.* When, exactly, does this thing run by? Or has it come and gone already and she missed it? She hears the front door opening downstairs. She closes the book, walks across the room, and puts it back on the shelf. She doesn't know why. She is standing at the window again when Erik comes into the room.

'Still here, Iz?' he says. 'I've bought some croissants. I hope you'll help me eat one or two before you go off somewhere.'

The sun has come out for a minute and it shines in the far window, the coffee has all gone, the croissants a distant memory, but Isabel and Erik are still in the living room. He has invited her to come to a jazz gig in a local pub and she has said yes. He has talked about his job in the university and the wonders of flexi-time. But most of all he has talked about his father, who died this year, about their reconciliation in the months before his death, the fact that his father still felt unable to meet Neil but had written him a long letter instead. Isabel asked some questions. Then they fell silent for a while. Now Erik speaks again: 'Your turn, Iz,' he says. 'I want you to tell me about the other man. Not the musician but the other one, the handsome one. I feel there was something there and you've not spoken about it.'

'I don't understand why you ask,' she says, without looking up.

'I'm possibly wrong but I thought something big had happened, something we aren't meant to talk about. OK, don't talk about it. Or do. There was a man, a landscape gardener or something. Didn't you work together on some project?'

Isabel lifts her eyes and looks steadily at Erik. He is essentially good-hearted, she thinks. They have never been that close and she knows his partner, Neil, very little at all. But she has a good feeling about Erik; he is trustworthy, dependable in a crisis. He doesn't fuss too much about anything. She takes a breath.

'It was an outdoor project for people with learning difficulties. He worked there and I was volunteering. There was a walled garden. Some woods. A sculpture trail of sorts.'

'This was what... about five years ago?'

'More. Six. Over six years ago. He was full-time. I only did one day a week. Daniel, that was his name, Dan was... well, he was attractive but I used the words *my boyfriend, Max*, in just about the first sentence I spoke to him and that settled things – it was easy, we could be friends. No flirting. It was summer and then it was late summer, September or something. I went one day a week to help out, except that the numbers had gone down, something to do with funding, and I wasn't really helping out but I liked being there...' She pauses, uncertain, not knowing where this is leading.

'Go on,' Erik says, quietly. He looks away and waits for her to speak.

'At the end, in the last few weeks, there was only one deaf

old man who came along. He liked best of all to sit and feel the sun on his face – he didn't want to do anything. Dan and I worked together, replacing panes of glass in an old greenhouse. We had to be physically close and careful and would also lapse into conversation quite a lot. I talked about my writing and he really listened and didn't think it was ridiculous at all. He showed me things. He was hard-working and indolent in turn. I told him about a Wordsworth poem where the poet sits under a tree all day...'

She looks towards the window and falls silent.

'Walt Whitman called himself *The Loafer,*' Erik says. 'Same thing. He would take a chair to sit on out in the woods or to the beach and he was proud of it. An honourable calling, I should say.'

Isabel turns to him again. 'When I left the garden in the afternoon he would say *cheers* or something and maybe there was some eye contact. I would drive off and straight away be thinking about the next time we would meet. An hour later I would be thinking of things I urgently wanted to say to him. I would feel quite a strong need to see him again. Do you really want to hear this stuff?'

'If you want to tell me.'

'I suggested that he came on this arty course at the Gallery. He had done some art in the past. He liked the city as much as he liked the countryside...'

'Whitman again. Sounds like a great guy.'

'Yes.'

'And you were just friends?'

'I was driving along one day with my sister, Petra. Dan was walking down the street. *Look, there's Daniel* I said and pressed the horn and waved. That was all I said, then there was a long silence. We got to the station where I was dropping her off and she asked about him. She knew it was something serious from the tone of my voice. She knew before I did. She knew we were more than friends.'

'So you and he came to the city as lovers?'

'No, it wasn't like that. It was as if we were in denial. We had hardly seen each other outside of his workplace.' Isabel speaks quietly. She isn't looking at Erik at all now.

'You came here and then what?' he asks. 'We never saw you, Neil and I were away on holiday. Lucy said something but she didn't know much. Have you been to Lucy's? Perhaps you've talked to her about it.'

'I've seen her.' Isabel's words are clipped short, as if she wants to bring the conversation to a close.

'Izzy, sweetheart,' Erik says. 'It's up to you. When you want to say more...' He looks at her sympathetically.

'I will talk about it sometime. Not now.'

Erik nods.

'Thank you,' she says.

'For what?'

'You know, for listening.'

They sit for a few moments longer. Then Erik gets up and goes out of the room. Time passes, Isabel doesn't know how much time, and then he puts his head around the door. 'I've got to go to work now,' he says. 'Take it easy, won't you?' He smiles, lifts his hand to say goodbye, and disappears from view. A little later she hears the front door closing behind him. She stays where she is for some time.

Isabel and Daniel are in the old rotating summer house in the corner of the walled garden. Wind and rain beat against the windows. There is no one else around. Their tea has gone cold. They have talked, grown silent, talked some more. The mood is that of easy companionship.

'You know the hill at the back of the village, the pointy one?' Daniel asks, for no obvious reason.

'Yes.'

'The pointy one?' he asks again.

'Yes. You asked and I answered,' she says, only mildly irritated.

'That's the thing,' he says. 'It's not pointy. If you look at it from the side, from the main road, it's just the end of a long ridge.' He smiles. He looks as if he has been proved right in some way.

'What are you saying?' she asks.

'Everything is different if you look at it from a different place.'

'Obviously.'

'I mean everything. Life is different.'

'Yes.'

'And you hope to some day find someone who sees things in the way you do – who stands in more or less the same place.'

She thinks for a moment. Sighs. 'I don't think it's ever like that, Dan. Not in my experience. But sometimes you can understand how someone else sees things. That's as good as it gets, I think. Literature seems like that to me. You get to see someone else's view of the mountain. You see it clearly enough to understand. Or you think you do.'

Daniel says nothing, smiles, looks at her closely. He leans his chair over to one side, reaches out, and draws something in the condensation on the window. Looks at Isabel again.

'A pointy hill,' she says.

'You see,' he says, triumphant but joking too. 'I don't have conversations like this with anyone else.'

'That might be a good thing.'

'I save things up tell you. You take the piss but I like telling you anyway. I felt this morning, when I was waiting for you to arrive... I felt as if I hadn't seen you for a long time.'

'It's Friday. I was here for a couple of hours on Monday morning. Four days.'

'I know.'

She smiles at him as if she will tease him again. She tries to speak with irony but it doesn't come out right. 'Long absence,' she says, and it sounds almost solemn.

They look at each other seriously for a moment. Then he smiles and they begin to laugh. They laugh because they understand each other perfectly. Or perhaps, and she can't help but think this, they laugh because they don't understand each other at all.

Sixteen

Daniel leaves the posh part of town and descends to the city centre with its heavy traffic and busy shops. He walks past the docks and takes a footbridge across the canal. He passes along some drab streets of two-up, two-down terraced houses and heads towards the grim dereliction of Paradise Road. He wonders about the relationship between affluence and altitude in the city; they seem to go together. And when he thinks of the house that he is staying in the words *low life* come to mind. It makes him walk more slowly; he is reluctant to spend another evening there. He crosses the road to check out a pub that might be OK. There is a poster in the window: *Jazz night tonight. The Tom Crouch Band.* That's it then, he will come back later, have a couple of pints, listen to the band for a while.

Now he is at the far end of Paradise Road, stepping over discarded chicken-and-chips wrappers and lager cans, walking around dirty puddles, watching out for the big cracks in the concrete pavement. On his left is a chain-link fence; behind that a yard and a workshop where a man is respraying a car. The fumes drift across towards him and he tries to hold his breath. An Alsatian dog comes running across from the workshop. It gets close to the fence, barks, growls, shows its teeth. Daniel is fine with this; he has seen it before, the I-would-tear-you-to-pieces-if-only-I-could-get-at-you bluff of a dog behind a fence. He carries on walking and the dog follows along. Then Daniel notices the open gate a few yards ahead. He wonders if the dog will dare to leave its territory or if it will pretend not to notice the lack of barrier. Daniel crosses the road and keeps on walking. The dog keeps level with him, reaches the gate, comes out onto the street. It's not barking now, its ears are back, its tail down. It makes a rush at him.

Daniel runs a few paces and the dog snarls and snaps at his legs. He feels the dog's teeth against his thigh, hears his jeans ripping, manages to keep moving. Then there is some shouting and the dog is slinking away. Daniel hears someone laughing. He stops and looks back. A man is standing by the door of the workshop watching him. He wears paint-stained overalls rolled down to his waist, a grubby white T-shirt, tattoos on his forearms, a tight, hard expression on his face. He's not a big man but he looks unpleasant. And he now has a nasty dog by his side. Daniel realises that he is shaking and wonders if it's fear or anger. The man looks at Daniel with hostility. He pats the dog on the head.

Daniel walks away; there is nothing else he can do. He is breathing very fast, feels very hot inside, knows that it's not fear. He has never felt so angry in his life, he is sure of that. He is not hurt; it's just tooth marks, torn jeans, and a certain amount of humiliation. It was the laughter that really got to him, the laughter and one of the words the man had called out. Perhaps he misheard. He doesn't think so. He hears the man's voice again, it replays in his head. A local accent, long rasping vowel sounds: 'Come here, Max, you stupid fucker.'

115

Some laughter. Then, 'Good dog. Well done.' More laughter and then, louder, so that he was sure of being heard, 'Very good dog, Max.'

ISABEL PHONE MAX. It was the first thing that Daniel saw when he came into the Gallery this morning, a sheet of paper sellotaped to the door, three big words written in thick felt-tipped pen, up there for everyone to see. Isabel, dutifully, has gone off to make conversation with the *complete bastard*, as Daniel refers to him. Meanwhile he tries to moderate his anger, tries to listen to Michael.

'This is what came in the post this morning,' Michael says. He is standing at the front of the room, holding a postcard up for everyone to see. 'It's from my daughter, Zoë, of whom I'm very proud, and who I miss very much. Take a look, everybody. What do you see?'

'Not very much,' Phil says, bluntly. 'Unless you want to pass it round. It's too small to see from here.'

'Too small,' Michael repeats. 'That's exactly it. She's away in France on a school exchange and having a good time, I hope, and we want to know all about how things are going and we only get these few words.' He allows himself a sad smile. 'But it's OK because it means she's not thinking of home and she's happy. But...' He looks away towards the window for a moment. 'But I guess it's all a part of being a parent. You miss them more than they miss you. It's fine.'

He pauses, scratches his head, puts his thoughts together, starts again.

'I caught the bus in this morning and walked the last bit and thought about sending a postcard back. Only I don't want to write, that's not my medium. I feel, today, like painting and printing and making marks in all sorts of ways on a giant postcard to say this is a giant message from me to you, Zoë. Wish you were here. This is what the city looks like to me this morning. Sunshine and showers, reds and yellows, blacks and blues. A crane with Dan at the top and Isabel at the bottom; Val, looking for her ley line; Phil, philosophising; the road-works on Doubleday Street; the new, glass-fronted building by the motorway reflecting the sky and the traffic. And much, much more.'

Michael stops and looks at the psychogeographers. 'Then I thought of you,' he says, and pauses for effect. 'You can imagine what I'm going to say next, can't you? Postcard time. Big as you want, we've got some old cardboard sheets downstairs, a bit rough but OK for poster paint and collage and so forth. Anyone not in the middle of something can paint a postcard home. How it looks, to you, today. Then maybe take some of your best stuff and use it to create a mind map. We'll cover a whole wall if we have to. What do you think?'

Some heads nod. Some feet shuffle backwards and forwards.

'I'll do one,' Phil says. 'What about yourself, Dan? Will you keep me company? Do you feel like sending a postcard to someone.'

'OK,' Daniel says, glad to take his mind off other things. 'I'll give it a go.'

Isabel comes in through the front door as Phil and Daniel reach the bottom of the stairs. Phil says nothing but goes on down the corridor to the storeroom and leaves them to it.

'Everything alright with the boyfriend, then?' Dan says.

Isabel doesn't speak but nods her head slightly, turns and

walks back out of the door. Daniel is not sure whether to follow or not. He knows that jealousy, anger and sarcasm are not particularly helpful at a time like this. He tries to control his feelings before following her.

He steps out of the door and stands still for a moment while his eyes adjust to the light. It is one of those days when big black clouds and bright sunshine follow each other across the city, darkness and brightness in turn, keeping people on their toes, making everyone feel very much alive. The water sparkles in front of him. The buildings opposite cast great blocks of shadow. There is the sound of traffic and church bells. To his left is the steel sculpture, *The Voyage*, a tree standing on either side of it, a wooden bench under the further one. Isabel sits there, staring at the water, waiting for him. He walks across and joins her.

'He's alright,' she says. 'But I think it's better if we don't refer to him as *the boyfriend*.'

'What did he want?'

'Just checking,' she says. She lifts her eyes to take in the city buildings spread out before them. 'Checking that I'm OK. Asking why my mobile is turned off. Checking up on me. He phoned the Gallery first thing this morning. He sends his regards.'

'I bet he does,' Daniel says. Then, more cheerfully, 'I promise I'll never ask you why your mobile's off.'

Isabel smiles. 'That's truly wonderful.' She lifts her hand as if to place it on his but changes her mind. 'Just be patient with me and don't get angry,' she says. 'I have to split up with this guy in my own time and in my own way. I have split with him in my head but it's more difficult than that. Max can take some handling.'

'Just phone him up and tell him that it's over. Why don't you do that?'

'I can't explain. It will happen. Just be patient.'

'There's stuff you're not telling me,' Daniel says, more sad than angry.

'No.'

'Then you're hedging your bets. That's not nice at all.'

'I'm not hedging my bets.'

'He told me in the pub that you had written erotic love poems to him.'

'That wasn't true.'

'No erotic poems?'

She doesn't answer straight away. She smiles. 'There was a poem.'

'Very good,' Daniel says, sounding bitter now.

'Max wasn't meant to see it. I pretended it was about him. It wasn't.'

'Who, then?'

She looks embarrassed, but not too embarrassed. 'It was just an idle thought, a scribble, something written without premeditation.' She turns towards him now. 'I've got a filthy imagination, I'm afraid. And I was already getting fond of you...'

Daniel is silent for a moment while he takes this in. He tries not to look too pleased with himself. 'What a wonderful woman you are,' he says. And, lowering his voice, 'I can't wait.'

'I think you might have to,' she says rather wistfully, her voice dropping to the level of his. 'There's nowhere we can be intimate together here. We're staying in a 200-bed youth hostel in the middle of town. And there are things I have to sort out. And it's very serious. It has to be special. When we sleep together it will be irrevocable.'

'What does that mean?'

'It means no turning back.'

They are silent now. A breeze picks up from the west, blows across the water, pushes a pile of dirty foam and litter against the quayside. Daniel gets to his feet.

'Where are you going?' she asks.

'Inside. I'm going to paint you a postcard. Wish you were here.'

'But I am here.'

'Then you can paint one for me too.'

Seventeen

Michael sits in a big armchair and looks across the room to his work in progress. His paintings and his mixed-media pieces are finished only when they are abandoned; until then they are left standing around to be looked at, fiddled with in one way or another, painted over perhaps. Sometimes a one-off piece of work gives rise to ideas that make it turn out to be the first in a series. It is important for him to take his time with them, to keep on looking.

He eases himself forward, fiddles with the cushion behind his back and manages to sit up straighter. Leaning against the wall opposite are his most recent works, the memory pieces: the painting of two people touching and the painting of two people not touching. The one of Isabel and Daniel; she is pointing out something to him, one hand touches his bare forearm. The one of himself and Christina before the split, turned away from each other, maintaining a distance. There are days when Michael desperately wants physical contact. Sexual pleasure, of course, he misses that. But as he gets used to that absence it is tenderness that he yearns for most of all. Looking from one picture to the other, from the almost-lovers to the un-lovers, simply makes him feel sad. Today he would like to be touched.

The phone rings and ends his reverie. He makes an unsuccessful attempt to get up, tries again and succeeds, limps across the room knocking over a half-empty teacup as he goes. He snatches up a paint-smeared cloth and dabs at the damp patch on the carpet. He reaches the phone as it stops ringing. He goes back to his chair and lowers himself back down. This is not a great day for him; he is mildly dysfunctional and not sure whether to be depressed or angry. If he felt steadier he would channel his energies into his work. Maybe later, he thinks.

He gets up again, moves more carefully across the room and switches on the answerphone.

'Hi, Michael. Christina here. Good news, Zoë's coming home. She won't say when but it's soon. There's a lot more but I don't want to tell you over the phone. What about Doubleday Street on Saturday? The cafe near the top, The Ferry is it called? Lots to talk about. Phone back.'

Michael phones back. No answer. He decides to go out about town. A brisk limp to get the blood circulating.

He feels much better as soon as he gets outside. The afternoon is bright with between showers sunlight. The colours are strong: the greens, yellows and browns of the leaves on the plane trees that line the street; the black tarmac; the patches of blue sky in the puddles. A soft breeze blows up from the west. On days like this he likes to think he can smell the sea.

He turns left and walks towards the Folly – not his usual route. Then he takes a right and follows a back street that runs parallel to the main road. He passes a church and a small burial ground and crosses the road when he gets close to the secondary school. He looks across at the portakabin class-rooms that now line the playground. And he thinks of Zoë.

She started school here before he had the flat and he came this way only when he was dropping her off or picking her up. He remembers that he found it hard to believe, for a while, that his little girl had grown big enough to enter such a place. And then, it happened so fast, she wasn't a little girl. She was a young woman, not speaking to her parents, going out with a complete loser, in and out of pubs and nightclubs, coming home (if she came home at all) at dawn. He and Christina were liberal parents but Zoë was too wild, too soon. She left school and left home at sixteen. At eighteen she moved further away, to another city. Nobody told him that it could happen as fast as that.

Michael is walking more quickly now, unaware of his surroundings, dipping into unwelcome memories. He crosses the road for no reason whatsoever, trips on a cracked paving slab, moves on. He thinks of the three-person silent family and the two-person silent family that followed. Christina and he ran out of things to say and things to do together. He made mistakes. It was after the Daniel and Isabel incident, or at least that's how it seems to him now; their stuff, the way they looked so good together, the way it went wrong with them, that was a catalyst, it changed him. He became dissatisfied and looked for love outside his marriage. He made mistakes. And then nobody would have anything to do with him. The one time that Zoë came home she failed to contact him and spoke only to her mother. This is why he doesn't normally come this way, past the school. It is all too much to think about.

And now there is the phone call: *Zoë's coming home.* Christina's voice had sounded positive – nothing bad has

123

happened. *There's a lot more but I don't want to tell you over the phone.* He won't try to guess what other news there is; he will see Christina in three days time and find out then. Meanwhile he starts to experience a range of powerful emotions: a certain nervousness, some sort of guilt, sadness, longing. But alongside all this he has a warm feeling too. For the first time in a while he feels that he has something to look forward to.

Eighteen

When Isabel phoned and asked Erik if she could stay for a few days he said that they would treat her as visiting royalty. *Minor royalty*, he said, *not head of state or anything. More like a princess than...* and he laughed when he realised where this was going, *more like a princess than a queen.* She felt cared for by the guys, an honoured guest, part of the family. And respected too. Now, in the crowded bar of the Oak Tree, they sit on either side of her, all three of them on a wooden settle against the wall, a table and drinks in front, a good view of the slightly raised area that serves as a stage tonight.

The pub is crammed full of jazz aficionados, a mixed crew: one or two students; one or two college lecturers; some old hippies; office workers; some practical people, builders, carpenters and suchlike. More men than women. All passionate about the music. Nobody drinking much, quiet during the sets, just nodding their heads or swaying a little to the beat. Then applauding enthusiastically; raising glasses and voices until the music begins again. The band is a three piece: a stocky, ponytailed man in a red T-shirt on drums and percussion; an older man, with swept-back hair and sports jacket, on keyboards; and the star of the show, Tom Crouch, on tenor and alto sax.

Isabel likes some of the music, is left behind by other pieces, listens and watches. She has drunk two pints of beer and now, feeling relaxed, has moved on to Scotch and ice. She takes small sips at the drink from time to time, enjoying the warm glow it gives. Her eyes are on the man at the front of the stage.

The saxophonist is a medium-height, medium-build, ordinary haircut, T-shirt and jeans young man. He is nervous every time he has to introduce a new tune, completely absorbed when playing, a little startled as he comes to the end. He plays with his eyes shut, moving unselfconsciously, lifting the instrument sometimes for emphasis, leaning forward for the deep, low-register runs. Each time he finishes a piece he opens his eyes wide and smiles shyly as if he has just awakened from a particularly good dream. A sexual dream, Isabel thinks, something cathartic.

No one speaks while he plays, they are more like an audience in a darkened cinema than drinkers in a pub. So Isabel is alone with the music and her thoughts. She watches the sax man. Now he is fast and funky, now cool, now clever, now slow and sensual. And every time he opens his eyes at the end of a piece... no, she shouldn't be thinking this. She feels the blood rise to her cheeks, tries to think of something else, sips at her drink.

There, he does it again. It's as if he has just finished running a race; he crossed the line in first position. Or he has just come to the surface after swimming under water. Or he is stepping down from a fairground ride. Or none of these things; it's something else. He has the look of a young man who has just fucked his girlfriend to a particularly fine orgasm. There, she has allowed herself to think it. And, next thought: lucky girlfriend.

She wonders if Erik or Neil find him sexy and were drawn here for that reason. But she knows they love jazz, Neil is especially serious about it. And the guy isn't that fantastic looking; he is ordinary. It's just the way he plays, the way he moves, the way he... oh no, here she goes again. Has someone spiked her drink? Is it the music? Something in the air? She doesn't normally get the hots for a complete stranger like this. Someone she hasn't even spoken to.

The band has started a new piece, a slower one. The drummer uses brushes to beat a soft rhythm. The keyboard player picks out a few chords, nothing flash. The sax man is playing a jazz standard, a tune Isabel more or less recognises. She watches him intently. It feels like voyeurism. So what? She is enjoying herself. She keeps on sipping at her drink, keeps on listening, keeps on watching.

The set is over, the musicians have packed up and people are getting ready to go.

'Let's move next door for a while,' Neil says.

Erik doesn't speak, just nods in easy-going compliance.

Isabel says, 'OK,' without thinking much about what is going on.

Neil picks up his beer and leads the way through to a smaller room where a handful of people have already settled down with refilled glasses. The door shuts behind them and she realises that the pub is closing and they have joined a private party. They settle down around a large table.

'Jazz club,' Neil says, anticipating her question. 'Members and invited celebrities, like yourself, only. It gives us a chance to go on past closing time. And we get to meet the band if they're not in a hurry to get away. But Tom's band are all locals anyway, they're always here. Local heroes, I think.'

The keyboard man is already sitting on a bar stool with a drink in his hand. The drummer has joined some friends at a nearby table. The saxophonist is at the bar but he turns and catches Neil's eye. He comes over to join them.

'Isabel, Tom. Tom, meet Isabel,' Neil says.

The man smiles and nods at her. She is as cool as possible, doesn't smile, glances at him and looks away. She knows that she has overdone the indifference and must appear rude but she can't do anything about that for the moment. The guys begin to talk among themselves. She tries to maintain an interest but doesn't really want to talk about music. It was good, that's all, she doesn't need to discuss the details.

She tries not to appear too interested in Tom Crouch. Perhaps she isn't. Now, without an instrument in his hands, he looks slightly more ordinary. He looks pale like someone who doesn't spend enough time outdoors. He looks tired. And he is not so young-looking close up: maybe late thirties, a little older than her. But he has a nice speaking voice, lower than she would expect, deep, somewhat resonant. There is something about him.

Time passes. Isabel fails to enter the conversation much despite the three men's polite encouragement. The keyboard player comes over and is introduced to her as Owen. A little later the percussionist and his girlfriend, Greg and Maria, join them too. Neil buys drinks for everyone and the atmosphere warms up. People are talking amiable nonsense and telling improbable anecdotes. They interrupt each other continually, laugh loudly, lean back on their chairs. Isabel begins to enjoy herself. Sometimes she catches Tom looking at her. She pretends not to notice. Then someone says something about circular breathing. She leans over towards the saxophonist and speaks to him, hoping, at last, to make up for her initial rudeness.

'The breathing thing – can you explain that to me?' she asks.

'I breathe in through my nose and out through the mouth at the same time,' he says. 'It shouldn't be possible but it is,' he shrugs. 'It allows me to play very, very long phrases. I try not to do it too often but save it for that special moment. But I have to do it a couple of times in every gig or I get into trouble with people like Neil. But it has to be right. A climactic moment.' He smiles at her. It's as if he's aware of some undercurrent of sexual innuendo in his words and he finds it funny and serious at the same time.

'You did it more than a couple of times tonight didn't you? The very long solos?' she asks.

He leans forward, as if to make himself heard above the general hubbub. 'It was a great gig. The Oak Tree audience is the best in the world. When I get famous I'll still come back here to play.'

'When you get famous?'

'That's right,' he says, quite seriously. 'That's how it's going to be. I know it sounds immodest but I work very hard at what I do. And I only mean famous in jazz terms. Notice I omit the word *rich* – that doesn't come with the job, I'm afraid.' Now he looks at her closely. 'Do you work hard at what you do?' he asks. 'I can imagine you doing something creative. Tell me all about it.'

He has expressed his confidence in his own abilities and now he turns his attention to her, implying that she is talented and creative too, part of a charmed circle. She is flattered. She notices that he has very dark eyes, chocolate brown irises, black pupils dilated in the poor light.

'I work at the hospital as a radiologist. I used to write but that seems to be in the past. I've had poems published. And a couple of short stories. I used to be very serious about it. Ambitious, like you are with your music.'

'What changed?' he asks, very focused on her.

'It seemed too self-indulgent. I wanted to do something for others and I trained as a radiologist. I put writing on the back boiler.'

'Self-indulgent? Well, I have to do music so there's no question. I couldn't do anything else. If it's self-indulgent that's just how it is. I plead guilty as charged, your honour. And I hope you still find time to write.' He thinks for a moment. 'Do you do free verse or metrical?'

'Both.'

'I'll tell you why I ask. I play piano too and I write songs. Only there are no words, I can't do that. I wonder if we could collaborate.' He gives her an intimate smile. 'I'm serious.'

A man comes over and puts a hand on his shoulder.

'Must I?' Tom asks. 'Can't it wait?'

The man whispers something in his ear.

'OK, boss. You're in charge,' Tom says. He gets up. 'He's my agent. I have to meet someone. But don't go away. Wait for me and think collaboration.' He manages a moment's eye contact before moving away across the room.

Isabel thinks collaboration and smiles; she's never heard it called that before. She looks around the room for Neil and Erik and finds that they are at the bar talking to the keyboard player and a couple of other people who she doesn't know. The table in front of her is crowded with empty glasses. The drummer and his girlfriend sit on the other side, turned towards each other, in their own little universe. Isabel is alone.

She watches Tom talking animatedly to a middle-aged couple in the corner of the room. Yes, he is attractive. And yes, she is drunk. And yes, she wants some collaboration. She believes it's on offer and it's what she needs tonight.

Some people have left and things are quietening down. She can hear background music, a jukebox or a sound system or something: Ella Fitzgerald and Louis Armstrong singing *What a Wonderful World*. Her mood changes. It's not the song that does it, she knows that. There is no reason, really, she just can't help herself. She begins to cry.

She gets a tissue from her bag and dabs at her eyes. She looks down at the glass on the table in front of her because she must look at something. She wonders why she is crying. It seemed, for a moment, that she might go to bed with an attractive stranger; that's a good thing isn't it? Now she feels that it would be cheating on someone else, someone she cares for very much. She has a very strong feeling about Daniel at the moment. But of course she does, she's been trying hard not to think of him all day.

She looks up and is lucky enough to catch Erik's eye. He can see that she's upset, he's wrapping up a conversation and will soon come over and take her home. She won't go to bed with a new man tonight because she won't be unfaithful to Daniel. She hasn't seen him for six years and she will never meet him again and their relationship never got started anyway. It's crazy, but that's how it is. There, Erik is coming over; he has a concerned expression on his face. Neil is looking towards her sympathetically. The sax man is busy being serious in the corner. And Daniel is a million miles away; that's the truth, isn't it? A million miles away and happily fucking someone else. Loving someone else, probably. And tonight she will be faithful to him.

Nineteen

Daniel steps into the hallway and slams the front door closed behind him.

'Fucking dog, shitting bastard fucking dog,' he says out loud, to no one.

He goes up to the bathroom, takes his trousers off and looks in the mirror. Teeth marks and bruising, red and purple, no broken skin. He goes through to the bedroom and puts on a clean pair of jeans. He is very angry and he doesn't know what to do about it. He is unsure about going to the pub tonight; someone might pick up on his mood and he could end up in an argument or worse, he can imagine it happening. He sits down on the end of the bed.

There is a noise of something hitting the back wall of the house, a scattering of small stones perhaps. Daniel doesn't care enough to find out what's happening; he puts his shoes on unhurriedly. It happens again and this time he gets up and goes to the window. His view from here is one part railway embankment and one part cloudy sky, nothing more. As he turns away he hears more stones hitting the wall and roof. He hears the crash of breaking glass. Now he moves very fast, downstairs and out of the back door, over the low brick wall, across the little plot of wasteland at the side of the house, through the pedestrian tunnel that leads under the railway and into the park. Five boys are coming down off the embankment and climbing over the fence. He feels very focused, his anger has an outlet and a direction. He runs towards them.

One of the boys sees Daniel, alerts the others, and they drop quickly off the fence and scatter. Daniel picks out the slowest one and chases after him. It's slightly uphill but Daniel sprints, powered on by adrenaline. He feels good. As he closes in the boy dodges and turns across the slope. He loses momentum and Daniel has caught up with him. He grabs him by the shoulder, spins him round, holds him tightly by the forearm. The boy is about eleven years old, not much more than half the height of Daniel, and very frightened. He doesn't attempt to struggle. Daniel stands and waits for his breathing to slow down. He had a few moments of exhilaration and now has a sense of impending anti-climax. Something has gone wrong.

He makes a decision and starts to drag the boy across the grass towards the tunnel under the railway. The boy lets himself be led; he has to trot to keep pace with Daniel. 'Where are you taking me?' he says. His voice is gruff, artificially deep, he is trying to sound older than he really is. He doesn't succeed.

Already Daniel's anger is subsiding but he carries on. 'We'll just take a little look at the mess you've made and then you can tell me what you're going to do about it,' he says.

At the entrance to the tunnel he lets go of the boy and pushes him on ahead. 'Don't think of running off,' he says. 'I can easily catch you again.'

Out on the other side the boy stops and waits to be told what to do.

'I live here,' Daniel says, pointing across the vacant plot to the house. 'The one with the broken window. Understand?'

The boy nods.

'What's your name?' Daniel asks, and his voice comes out softer than he intended.

'Tom.'

'Tom what?'

The boy is still scared but he looks up at Daniel defiantly.

'Tom Crouch. And I didn't do anything.'

'You just happened to be there. Is that right?'

'Yes.'

'I don't believe you.'

Daniel becomes aware that a man is crossing the road towards them. He is short, wears work boots, jeans and a donkey jacket, looks concerned. He walks up and stops a few paces away. 'What's going on?' he asks.

'Not much,' Daniel says.

The man addresses the boy, 'What's this all about, Ben?'

The boy holds his head down and tries to avoid his father's gaze.

Daniel finds that his anger has now completely dissipated. He feels sorry for the boy. 'He was one of a group of lads throwing stones down from the railway line,' he says. 'He was the slowest so I caught him.'

The man is angry, confused and weary. He looks at his son for a long time without speaking to him. He turns to Daniel. 'He's been in trouble before,' he says. 'The police have been involved a couple of times.' He shakes his head. 'I don't know what to do, I really don't.'

'They broke a window,' Daniel says. 'Perhaps we should take a look at that?'

'OK,' the man says. He follows him across the patch of waste ground and into the backyard. The three of them stand in front of the little kitchen extension and examine the damage. The bigger window is OK but the small side one is broken.

'This will make a hole in your pocket money, Ben,' the man says.

'Not Tom, then?' Daniel asks. 'Tom Crouch?'

'He's called Ben Walcott and I'm Pete Walcott. I'd like to say I'm pleased to meet you but I'm not. I'm sorry about that. And Tom Crouch lives on the next road up. He's a good bloke, a musician, doesn't break windows.'

'I'm Dan Brownlow,' Daniel says offering his hand for the man to shake.

Without saying more the two men begin to work together clearing up the glass from the floor and from the edges of the window frame. The boy stands awkwardly in the corner of the yard, watching. Daniel finds a piece of damp hardboard in the outdoor toilet, cuts it to size with a bread knife and wedges it in place as a temporary repair. Pete Walcott agrees to come back with a piece of glass as soon as possible. He and his son are leaving by the front door when a police car pulls up.

A uniformed officer steps out. 'Excuse me, sir,' he says, addressing Daniel, who happens to be standing nearest to him. 'We've had a report of a vandalism incident. Kids on the railway line. You don't know anything about it by any chance?' His manner is polite but arrogant, slightly threatening.

Daniel glances at the father and son standing beside him. Neither of them look surprised. The son has a hard expression on his face. The father looks resigned, defeated.

'No,' Daniel says. 'I've not heard anything.'

The policeman waits for more.

'I'm sorry we can't be of any help,' Daniel says.

The policeman looks at the three of them critically, as if trying to work out a puzzle. Then his radio begins to make a noise. He gets back into the car and drives off without saying anything more.

It is eight o'clock in the evening and Daniel sits on a bench in the park. The ground drops away in front of him down to a fence, beyond which is the railway embankment. Daniel can see the upstairs windows of the houses on Paradise Road and, over the rooftops, the lights of the city. He is thinking about the jazz night at the local pub. He might drop in and check it out. He might not.

He has just had a supper of microwave pizza and chips at the Walcotts'. It was awkward but the father asked him to join them and he accepted. It seemed the right thing to do. There were only the three of them, Pete Walcott, Ben, himself; no brothers or sisters and no Mrs Walcott either. Daniel didn't ask. The important thing, Pete Walcott said, was that his son understood that other people really existed. The people whose car or house you were smashing up, they might be coming round to dinner later on. You had sit with them at the same table. That was all; he couldn't explain it any more than that. The boy got up and apologised to Daniel as he was leaving. He wasn't asked to but he did. It felt like something had been achieved.

Daniel sits on the bench and looks at the city. He feels cold but he is no hurry to go anywhere. It has been a long day and he has some things to turn over in his mind. This morning he was in the posh part of town following a smartly dressed woman who reminded him of someone from his past. He thinks about Isabel now, not because he can't help himself but because he consciously, deliberately, turns his thoughts towards her. She is probably far away and she is not thinking about him, of that he can be sure. She is nursing a baby or writing a poem or chatting up some handsome prat in a wine bar or hosting a dinner party. Or she is in another time zone; she is stepping into a warm sea or climbing a high hill covered with snow. Or she is having her teeth filled or buying mangoes or... fuck knows what she's doing but she isn't thinking of him, why should she after all this time?

Reasons for not going to the pub and listening to the Tom Crouch Band: number one, he would have to pass by that vicious dog again; number two, he's thinking about Isabel and the whole business makes him feel miserable as hell, he can hardly face a room full of smiling, happy, pissed-up faces in this state; number three, as if the other reasons weren't enough, he doesn't like jazz, he never has done.

Twenty

Michael watches the psychogeographers at work and he feels good. They are more than halfway through the project and things have really taken off. Socially it's a success; it is such an eccentrically diverse group of people that there is no chance of cliques forming and no way anyone can feel themselves to be an outsider. They all laugh a lot and they take the piss out of each other, and him, in a good-natured way. And they have loosened up; everyone is trying new things, pushing at the boundaries of what they can do and who they are.

The postcard idea was about as spontaneous as you can get. Michael had walked into the room and started spouting the things that were on his mind and most people picked up on it. Phil and Daniel got some huge cardboard boxes out of the storeroom and cut them up. Now Phil has covered a large postcard with twenty-five smaller ones, each inscribed with a piece of graffiti that he has collected from the city's public toilets during the last few days. He has reproduced (accurately, he says) pornographic drawings as well as writings in a cheerful range of colours. The piece is called *Come Again?* Freddie and Esther are making a six-foot-long cityscape collage out of imagination and litter (quite a leap away from their usual medium of watercolour). Val is making some postcards with drawings of the pagan sacred sites of the area as they were, she believes, before the city came into existence. Phil has pointed out that her standing stones are just as horny as some of his drawings. It says something about the nature of her imagination.

Isabel has drawn a large panorama with simple outlines of buildings and groups of buildings and is filling in the spaces with stream-of-consciousness poems. She thinks it doesn't really come off (Michael secretly agrees with her) but finds it cathartic. Daniel is covering a large postcard with home-made stamps, each one a quick sketch of Queen Isabel, drawn from life. Michael thinks that they are good; viewed together the drawings make up a lively narrative portrait. He doesn't say anything to Daniel because he thinks it will make him self-conscious.

Michael feels he is halfway to being redundant now that everyone is getting on so well. He is tempted to start some work of his own, maybe make a few sketches. His thoughts are interrupted by the arrival of the man from the front desk downstairs.

'There's someone on the phone asking for Isabel Davies,' he says to Michael. 'She's not up here by any chance?'

'Did you catch his name?' Michael asks.

'Max something or other. I said I couldn't leave the desk but he phoned up again and started getting bolshy.'

'You'd better go down,' Michael says. 'I'll get her for you.' He looks across at Isabel and Daniel. She is writing something in a notebook now; he is sketching her profile. Michael doesn't want to disturb them but feels he must. He walks over.

'Someone on the phone for you, Isabel,' he says. 'I'm afraid it's Max again.' He hesitates for a moment before adding, 'I could tell him you're not here.'

'Yes,' she says, suddenly sitting up straighter. 'Thank you. You could tell him I'm out all day.' She gives him a sad smile.

The man from the front desk has gone already and Michael plods on down after him. He has nothing against Max really but finds that he has taken sides with Isabel and Daniel and he is enjoying making Max wait. When he gets as far as the bottom staircase he hears someone coming down fast behind him and stands aside. Daniel mutters a thank you as he passes. When Michael reaches the ground floor Daniel is at the desk holding the phone out in front of him as if it is something deeply distasteful. He turns towards Michael.

'He put the phone down,' he says. 'He wouldn't speak to me, the stupid cunt...' He stops himself too late.

Isabel has reached the bottom of the stairs now and she stands and looks at him critically. Something about her manner suggests disappointment as much as anger. There follows a short period of silence that feels like it goes on for ever. The man at the desk gets up, walks over to the window and looks out.

'I'm sorry,' Daniel says, eventually.

'And he's the stupid one?' Isabel says. 'You're not stupid at all are you, Dan?'

She turns away and walks back up the stairs.

Daniel looks towards Michael as if asking for help. Then he sets off after Isabel. He climbs the stairs slowly, in no hurry to catch up with her.

When Michael reaches the third floor again he sees that Isabel is talking to Val. She has turned her back towards the corner of the room where she and Daniel were working a few minutes ago. Daniel is there again, carefully taking down the sketches of her that he had Blu-tacked to the giant postcard. Michael starts towards him as if he will say something sympathetic or supportive. He changes his mind and sits down on a randomly placed chair.

Isabel and Daniel are at opposite corners of the room and it feels like everybody else is aware of it. The psycho-geographers are talking quietly or not at all. Michael has been to livelier funerals. He watches Isabel cross the room and approach Daniel.

'I think we should work separately this afternoon,' she says. 'I have things I need to do.'

'OK,' Daniel says and he turns away from her. He carries on taking down the drawings and stacking them carefully into a neat pile.

Isabel picks up her bag and walks out of the door.

Michael sits at the back of a small cafe in the city centre and eats sausages, chips and beans. He had wanted to sit at the table by the window but when he came back from the counter it had been taken by a young couple. He takes a sip of his tea and tries not to look at them. He is irritated by the fact that they sit by the window but don't want to look out of it. Yes, they are that type of couple; they are at the *only have eyes for you* stage of the relationship. He slices his sausages lengthways so that they cool down more quickly. He puts his fork through a chip and smears it with tomato ketchup. He looks up and sees the woman nodding her head enthusiastically at something her lover has said.

An unpleasant thought drifts to the surface of Michael's mind. He looks away from the couple and down at his food again. It suddenly occurred to him, just for a passing moment, that their happiness is undeserved and that things will go wrong for them. Worse than that, he almost wishes for things to go wrong. What a bitter, selfish man he is turning into. He is very much aware that he didn't used to be like this; he had always wanted the best for the people around him. He was always on the side of young lovers and not-so-young lovers too. So what's happening to him?

He eats his lunch slowly and thinks it through. When he strayed from the marriage bed he found himself unsure of whether to tell Christina hurtful truths or kind lies, did both, and suffered the consequences. Their marriage ended five years ago. The years that followed were difficult and he was lonely sometimes. He particularly missed contact with his daughter. But then there was always the hope of new romance. That was on his mind much of the time. It kept him feeling positive. And, while the relationship that broke up his marriage ended soon enough, there were a couple of other brief flings.

The couple are talking animatedly. Their food has arrived but they seem unaware of it and are letting it go cold. Michael knows that they will eat a few mouthfuls each, leave the rest, and think nothing of it at all. He remembers that between his romantic flings there was always hope and sometimes anticipation. But his present situation... he doesn't want to think about it; he's frightened of where his thoughts will lead him. The truth is, perhaps, that he is unavailable for relationships now. Who would want a lover who will be a dependent in a few years time? And if he really cared for someone would he wish that on them? No, of course not. If he ever thought he was growing close to someone again the kindest thing would be to quietly back away. And that, he guesses, is why he is so envious of other people's happiness.

He looks at the couple by the window, eating their lunch but with their eyes on each other most of the time. He thinks of Isabel and Daniel; he wanted good things for them and he did his best. What would he do now in a similar situation? He doesn't know. He only feels like turning his back on others, leaving them to it; it's not his business to get involved. He knows that he used to be different from this. The Michael Marantz sitting in the cafe right now, the miserable joyless old bastard with a half-eaten plate of sausages and chips in front of him, this is not who he wants to be.

Twenty-one

Isabel and Val have visited a cafe and three charity shops. Isabel bought a cotton dress that she probably won't wear until next summer and a book of poems by local writers. Val bought a cardigan and a porcelain pig. Then they wandered, in the random way that Michael has encouraged, and have come to a park with poplar trees, a children's playground, and, in the corner by the railway bridge, a water maze. They have cleared out the fallen leaves and crisp packets so that the water can flow freely. It emerges from a brass spout at the centre of the maze and passes back and forth along little channels between the brickwork until it reaches the edge and disappears down a drain.

Now Isabel sits on a bench and watches Val make a little paper boat and set it on the water. It gets stuck from time to time and she pokes it with a stick to keep it moving. When it gets too soggy to float she gives up.

'Pip and Rudy would love this,' she says, stepping across the bricks towards Isabel. 'Pip most of all. He could play here for hours.'

'Pip is your youngest?' Isabel asks.

Val nods. 'Eight next month. God, I do miss him when I'm in a place like this. It's wonderful to have a break from them but it's painful too. I wish they were both here now. If John could bring them here to play for an hour and then take them away again, or even if he didn't take them away again, it would be brilliant.' She sits down next to Isabel. 'Of course we live too far from here but you know what I mean. If it was possible...'

Isabel thinks of Val as a cheerful person, sane in a crazy sort of way. A strong bedrock of contentment lies beneath her momentary sadness, that's how it seems to Isabel. It contrasts with her own state of mind, shaky on the surface and shaky deep down too. She doesn't speak for a moment because she doesn't know what to say.

'You still mad at Dan?' Val asks.

'Yes, I am,' Isabel says, hesitantly. 'I'm very fond of him, you know that. But maybe he's impossible, too much of a big kid in some ways. The crane thing, for instance. And when I tried to get him to promise not to do anything like that again he just said *no*. Very simply and very honestly *no, I can't promise*. And this morning, the phone business with Max. I had no idea he would do that, just rush downstairs and try to speak to him. God knows what he was going to say. The funny thing is I don't think he knew he was going to do it either. Even a couple of seconds beforehand he didn't know. Do I really want to be with someone like that? I'm not sure sometimes.'

'I think you are pretty sure,' Val says, smiling.

Isabel lapses into silence again.

Val gets up and walks around the outside of the maze, picks a leaf out of the water, comes back and sits down. 'He'd make a good dad,' she says. 'If you're after a long-term bloke you might think of that. But I know it doesn't work that way.'

Isabel still says nothing.

'Izzy, for fuck's sake, what's going on with you? Dan tried to speak to Max on the phone and called him a rude name when he hung up. That's about par for the course, that's how men are. It's not enough to upset yourself about for long.'

'No, I suppose not.'

'What is it, then?'

'There is something else,' Isabel says, tentatively. 'You have to promise not to tell anyone.'

'I promise.'

'I think I might be pregnant. I've been trying not to think about it. You know how it is, you get a niggling little worry if you're a few days late but you try to put it out of your mind for a bit. But it's more than a week.'

'You're in a strange place, Iz. It'll be alright when you get home.'

'I'm not so sure. I get worried. And I start thinking all sorts of things. I can't have a baby right now. I just can't.'

'Have you spoken to Dan about it?'

'No way,' Isabel says, sounding alarmed. 'He mustn't know.'

'But...' Val is hesitant. 'But it would be his, wouldn't it?'

'No. Dan and I have never slept together.'

'Why ever not?' Val says, obviously surprised.

'Because we're just starting out. And there's Max. And it's all rather serious.'

Val thinks it through for a moment. 'You haven't told Max?' she asks.

'Absolutely not. He mustn't know either. Because I won't have his child, I'd rather have an abortion. There, I've said it, I would rather have an abortion. Even if Dan wasn't around I still couldn't have a child with Max. He wants us to and that's why he must never know. He wants it for the wrong reasons. It would make our relationship permanent in his mind. It would bind us together.'

A couple of middle-aged dog walkers come around the bend in the path and walk towards them. Isabel and Val wait quietly for them to pass out of hearing.

'You might have to get it sorted then,' Val says.

'You make it sound easy.'

'No, it's not easy at all and I know because I've been there.' Val is speaking very quietly now. 'One abortion. I was fifteen at the time. And two miscarriages. So I know that you can go through it and come out the other side. Have you had a pregnancy test?'

'It's too early, isn't it?'

'No it's not too early. For God's sake, Iz, have a test first and then you can worry afterwards if you have to. We'll see if we can find a chemist that's still open, OK?'

'Yes, of course, you're right. It's just that I've been thinking all sorts of things.'

'Like what?'

'Things like *I want a baby and I don't care who the father is.* I have never thought anything like that before. And then I think *no, that's the last thing in the world I need.* And then I think about Dan and I just want to go to bed with him as soon as possible.'

'That last one sounds like the best idea to me.' Val smiles and nods in encouragement.

'And there's another thing...'

'Which is?'

'I came here to write. It's a bit more than a hobby for me. I'm very serious about it.'

Val shakes her head and laughs. 'Honestly, that sounds like the least of your worries. Hey, why don't you think of this week as a time for collecting material. You know, research.'

Isabel smiles. She feels better just by talking about it all. And she likes the way Val doesn't get too solemn about things. A man walks past with a large poodle on a lead. A group of teenage lads come by on skateboards. The two women watch quietly for a while.

Then Isabel breaks the silence. 'You know the bottle sculpture by the Gallery,' she says. 'You look inside and it's like an old film or something. A sepia-tinged cabin on an old cruise liner. Well, I want to get in there. It's impossible but I want to get in that cabin and lie down on the bed and float away from it all.'

'Who would be there with you, Iz?'

'I'd be alone.'

'Are you sure?'

Isabel doesn't answer straight away. Her eyes lose focus as if she is already floating away in her imagination. 'Alone and at peace,' she says. 'My mind at rest. And when I'm ready there's a polite knock on the door. *Come in* I say and the door opens slowly...'

'And who's there?'

Isabel turns her head and smiles. 'It's Daniel, of course it is. Who else could it possibly be?'

Twenty-two

Daniel spent two lunchtime hours in the pub with Phil, Freddie and Esther. He drank too much and resolved to walk it off with an afternoon ramble about town. He was told off for pissing against a tree in a churchyard; fell asleep on a park bench and woke up shivering because the sun had gone behind the clouds; got lost in an endless suburb; took a bus back into the town centre; got off without paying and was nearly run down by a cyclist.

Now it is early evening. He walks into the foyer of the youth hostel as Isabel reaches the foot of the stairs and he blurts out the words that have to be said, that he has been repeating to himself much of the afternoon.

'I'm sorry. I apologise. I did the wrong thing and I said the wrong thing. I'm sorry.'

Isabel looks confused, as if her thoughts are elsewhere and she can't understand what he is saying.

He hesitates for a moment and then tries again. 'I was stupid, I know. I'm sorry I tried to speak to Max on the phone and I'm sorry about my choice of vocabulary. I didn't mean to be offensive.'

Isabel doesn't reply and he has no idea what is on her mind, what effect his words are having on her. So he goes on, 'It's difficult for me that you're still going out with him.'

'OK,' she says, without much expression in her voice.

'Don't you see he's my rival or something. I'm not going to be best mates with him. I think he's a prat. And I think he's no good for you.'

'I see.'

'Do you?'

She shakes her head. 'I don't know anything at the moment, Dan.'

They fall silent and they both realise that they are still standing in the middle of the foyer and that people are obliged to walk around them.

'Let's go somewhere,' he says.

She nods and follows him out of the door. They cross the street and walk over to a bench by the water. They sit down awkwardly.

'Do you understand how it is for me?' he asks.

'No, I don't. I can't imagine. I'm sorry,' she says, not sounding remotely apologetic.

'I try not to hate Max.'

'Good. He's not a complete shit, as you seem to think. And he's part of my experience. You'll have to accept that. If you think he's crap then where does that leave me? What sort of person does that make me?'

'Misguided. Someone who made a mistake.'

'No,' she says hesitantly. 'Max was not a mistake. He was... is a special person and I was with him for good reasons.'

'And I'm fed up with hearing what a great guy he is.'

'You sound angry.'

'That's about right. I try not to be but I feel like I'm being led up the garden path. You are...' he can't find the right word for a moment. 'You're significant to me. You're important, you're special, a big part of my world. Central, maybe.'

He waits for some response to this but she doesn't speak and she doesn't turn her head towards him.

'I try to be patient,' he says, a hard edge to his voice now. 'I try not to get angry with him. With you.'

'I'm sorry,' she says. 'I've got a lot on my mind.'

He waits again for her to say more but she won't even look at him. Her silence, her stillness, seem like a rejection. He can't read her body language. He can't believe that she is giving him so little. It crosses his mind that she is silently crying but in the fading light it is difficult for him to tell. If only she would say something.

'I wonder if perhaps I have been making a mistake,' he says. 'A stupid, stupid mistake.'

Isabel says nothing to correct him. She appears to be in a state of shock, incapable of speech. He waits for her to say something but she doesn't. He gets up and walks away.

Daniel is running. He is inappropriately dressed for this: jeans, T-shirt, a woollen jumper, beaten-up old trainers with all the bounce gone out of them. He sweats heavily. But it is the right thing to do, it will make him feel a little better. He runs along the path beside the canal, still water on his left, iron railings and a disused railway line on his right. He walked away from Isabel and then he started to run, too quickly at first, now loping along at a comfortable pace.

On the bank opposite him are the arse ends of small factories and warehouses in various stages of dilapidation, all spewing out rubbish onto the mud. A burnt-out car has somehow made its way onto the railway track. His path is littered with broken glass and dog shit. Above him the sky is patchy grey, overcast in the west where the setting sun might be. It is growing darker by the minute and there is no one else around. The landscape through which he moves appears blighted, forlorn and colourless.

Daniel runs because it is the best thing for him to do. He would like to shout obscenities, fight someone, or break something. He would like to cry. But running soothes him and his anger is falling away. He loves Isabel. There, that's the word he hasn't used until now, not in his thoughts and not out loud. But it's true. It's true and it's intense and right now it's very painful. Perhaps things will turn out right; he knows that's possible. But if everything goes to shit he knows what to do. He will run and he will keep on running until he is a very long way away.

Twenty-three

Michael limps up Doubleday Street towards the new outdoor clothing shop on the corner. He needs some warm things for the autumn and the winter that will follow: a jumper that doesn't have holes in the elbows, a couple of thick lumberjack shirts, a new pair of trousers. This morning he feels rough and he knows that he looks rough too. He hasn't shaved for three days and his stubble is heavy and peppered with grey; at his age it makes him look like a tramp. His eyes are red and his face is drawn from lack of sleep. He was woken in the night by tremors and twitches in his limbs and, for the first time, in the muscles of his face. And when his body settled down his mind started working overtime. He thought about Zoë, about her contacting Christina but not him. It made him feel jealous and sad. He understands the reasons but he is upset anyway. In the early hours of the morning he got up and switched on the radio; the world service of the BBC. He listened to a documentary about the punk years until they played a song with the words *no future* in the chorus. In the middle of the night, in some discomfort and feeling rather sorry for himself those words seemed horribly appropriate to his circumstances.

He reaches the top of the street and turns into the new

shop. He trips up on the slight rise in ground level at the doorway and enters staggering and nearly falling over. It is only just nine o'clock and the place is empty apart from the two young male shop assistants. They have both noticed him and they exchange knowing looks before turning away and pretending to be unaware of his presence. He walks over to a display of mountaineering equipment, not because he is likely to go mountaineering ever, but because it is close to the door and he needs to pull himself together. He studies the ropes, ice axes and caribiners and thinks of simply stepping back out onto the street and going home again. And then what will he do? No, he must make the best of it and get something done this morning. He knows that there are people in the city coping with greater difficulties than his.

He wanders around the shop looking at winter coats and jumpers and shoes. The clothing rails seem to be very close together and it is difficult for him to avoid knocking things onto the floor as he passes. First it is a waterproof. He picks it up and puts it back on the rail. Then it is a fleece jacket. His foot is resting on one corner of the jacket and he can't understand at first why it is hard to lift it off the floor. Then he steps back and manages to return the thing to its place. A large group of students is coming into the shop now. That's good; it will make him less conspicuous. He limps over to the display of work shirts and takes a look. He picks out one that is the right size and a reasonable colour and hangs it on the end of the rail.

One of the shop assistants comes over to keep an eye on him. Michael tries to ignore the young man but senses something confrontational in his manner, a rudeness or even arrogance in his body language. He tries to carry on with what he is doing but is getting deeply irritated. Then he finds that he has come to a standstill, his hands hanging loosely by his sides.

'Can I help you, sir?' the young man asks, not sounding helpful at all but actually slightly aggressive.

'Fuck off,' Michael mutters under his breath.

'I'm sorry, sir,' the man says in a tone of calculated irony.

'I said *fuck off*,' Michael says, louder this time.

His hands are shaking and it is clear that this morning has been a disaster. He just wants to leave but the man is blocking his path and calling for his colleague to come over. Now they are on either side of him. They take an arm each and firmly escort Michael to the door. He feels that he is in no condition to resist. At the entrance to the street they release him and one of them bends to speak in his ear.

'Come back when you're sober,' he says.

Michael is part way down Doubleday Street, cheering himself a little with the thought that he might go back to the shop, but at night-time, with a sledge hammer, when he hears a voice he recognises.

'Hello Mike, long time no see. How's it going?'

'Tony, very good to see you. I hope you're having a better day than I am.'

They move to the edge of the pavement to let people pass by.

'What's up, mate?' Tony asks. 'You look like death warmed up. Only less cheerful, if you don't mind me saying so.'

'I was thrown out of a shop for being drunk,' Michael says. 'Which is unlucky, as I'm stone-cold sober.' He goes on to tell him about his morning so far.

Tony listens to the story sympathetically. 'Was there anything in particular you wanted?' he asks. 'I can go in and get it for you.'

'No, it's alright. Really.'

'Sure?'

Michael considers. He doesn't want to go home empty-handed. 'There was a shirt, a blue work shirt. I hung it at the end of the rail. Forty-two inch chest...'

'Stay where you are, Mike. Consider it a done deal,' Tony says and sets off up the street. He comes back quite soon with a bag containing not one but two shirts of the right size. They walk on together downhill, towards the docks.

'How much do I owe you?' Michael asks.

'No, really. My treat.'

'But I have to. How much were they?'

Tony looks sideways at him and grins.

'You didn't...'

'You didn't think I was going to pay for them did you, Mike? After the way they treated you.'

Michael laughs out loud, happier now than he would have thought possible earlier on.

They carry on together without speaking for a while. They reach the point where their paths diverge and stop for a moment before parting.

'You know that thing you got?' Tony asks.

'Parkinson's.'

'That's the one. It's bad, I know.'

'It's pretty awful.'

'I hope you don't mind, Mike, but I've been asking people about it. I brought the subject up in the pub and it seemed like everybody knows someone who's got it. Most of them are older than you, of course. But there's this bloke, Johnny Cash we call him, there's a story to that name but you don't need to know. Well, Johnny's brother has had it for years, twenty years or something, and it's getting worse. He was on the plane to Malaga – they've got a little place down there and that's another story we won't be telling. Anyway he's on the plane and he's scared of flying and it makes his symptoms come on. All of a sudden his leg starts shaking, he can't control it, can he? And his leg is rubbing up and down against this woman's leg who's sitting beside him. Are you with me?'

Michael nods his head.

'He tried to explain but she was having none of it. Called the air hostess, she did. Ask me how it all turned out.'

'How did it turn out?'

'They took immediate action. Humiliating, it was.'

'What happened?'

Tony grins. 'They put him in first class. Free drinks, special menu, the works. He thought about trying it on the way home.'

Michael smiles to himself. 'That's a very good story,' he says. 'I need to hear a few more like that. You say he'd had it twenty years?'

'Something like that. They said it can be very slow.'

'Tony, I owe you one.'

'It was a pleasure.'

'Not for the shirts so much but for the story. Sometimes it gets me down and I need to hear stuff like that.'

'I know you do, Mike. That's why I saved it up for you. It's true, like. It's a true story. And when I heard it I thought I'd pass it on to you. Johnny's brother gets a lot of pain with it too; I'm not saying it's a laugh a minute. But he smokes plenty of dope and that seems to help. But what I'm saying is... well, it's not the end of everything, is it?'

'No. Thanks for that, Tony. You're right. It's not the end of everything.'

Twenty-four

Ten o'clock in the morning of Isabel's fifth day in the city. She sits at the table in Erik and Neil's beautiful living room, a pile of estate agent's printouts in front of her, a cup of coffee, now cold, to one side. She is thinking about Daniel. If she ever met him again she would ask this question: *Why did you run away from me when I needed you most of all?* She tries to imagine his answer.

She has found that she is willing to think about those few days now. In fact it seems wrong not to do so; the events, and non-events, of that period changed her life. And she will try to understand; her anger and her contempt have diminished over the years. She wants to think about what made Daniel do that, what it was like for him. She speaks aloud into the empty room.

'Why did you run away from me when I needed you?'

Silence.

Then a voice in her head. 'Because I didn't know. Because you were with Max.'

And so she lets herself imagine that they have met up again after all these years. He has a lot of explaining to do. A dialogue begins.

'How are things with you?' she asks.

'Fine,' he says. 'And yourself?'

'I'm well.'

They are being careful of each other, uncertain how to progress.

'And Max?' Daniel asks. 'Is he alright?'

'I don't know. I haven't seen Max for some years.'

'Good.'

'Yes. That's right. Good.'

'I thought I saw you in the street,' the imaginary Daniel says. He is more relaxed now. He smiles. 'It was a boy with hair the way you had yours then. I saw him from behind in a crowd. Just head and shoulders. I called out your name. When I got closer I saw it wasn't you. Pretty stupid, eh?'

'I smelled you once. I was sitting on my own in a room. Not at home but in someone else's house. I wasn't thinking about you but you were suddenly there. I don't know what brought that on.'

'I dreamed that you had a baby. It was OK. It was like a miniature person, not a baby at all.'

'I dreamed that you were at my parents' house. You were in the garage fixing my car.' She pauses. 'Dan. What are you doing here?'

'Dreaming.'

'That sounds right. That's how I remember you. Always the dreamer. Why did you run away from me when I needed you most?'

'Because of the accident. Because you were with Max.'

'I called at your place but they said that you'd gone away somewhere.'

'I wrote but you never answered. So I went off.' He shrugs.

'I didn't get any letters from you.'

'I sent them.'

'Maybe it was Max. He probably intercepted them. He was awful at that time.'

Daniel changes the subject. 'I saw Michael the other day but we didn't speak. I liked that man. He was on our side.'

'It was six years ago.'

'We will always refer to it as *the six years*. You know, the gap between then and now.'

'We'll *always* refer to it?'

He considers for a moment. 'Yes, I think so. Always.'

Isabel directs a smile into the empty room. She shakes her head and laughs out loud. Her face wears an expression of wry amusement and sadness and resignation.

Maybe it would be like that if they met again, she thinks. No anger and no recriminations. A simple explanation for what happened. They could be friends or perhaps something more. It doesn't do any harm to dream about it once in a while. It seems very unlikely that it will ever happen.

Twenty-five

It is nine o'clock in the morning and the psychogeographers are in the top room of the Gallery waiting for Michael to turn up and give them direction and encouragement. There are some smiles and laughter. There is some nursing of hangovers and drinking of coffee. Everybody seems to be having a good time except Daniel. He sits in the corner watching the others, feeling crap, wondering where Isabel has gone. She sat with Val at breakfast time and didn't want to speak to him. She ate very little and then suddenly got up and walked out. That was the last he saw of her. He could walk across the room to Val now and ask if Isabel is OK but he doesn't. He doesn't feel like doing very much at all.

Michael comes in, claps his hands, starts his morning spiel.

'*Tout le monde*,' he says. '*Ecoutez bien*. Listen up. A few words while we're all together in one place. Today is the penultimate day as you know and we all need to do something good. Tomorrow we go to the Little Red Lighthouse, we'll be setting off in the minibus about now, back for lunch. So today is your last full day here to get on with your own stuff. Use it wisely.'

He is interrupted by a stifled guffaw from Phil.

'Well, not necessarily wisely, that's the wrong word. But, you know... let's make the most of it. I've heard the weather forecast and it's going to be heavy showers and short intervals of sunshine. Outdoors might be a bit dodgy. Can't think of anything more to say. Ask me a question someone.'

'Tell us about the Little Red Lighthouse,' Phil says.

'Little Red... well, I don't want to say too much. I don't want to spoil it for you.'

He turns away from them, walks to the window and looks out. Something in his body language says *I haven't finished yet* and they wait for him to continue. He turns to face them again.

'OK,' he says. 'I was once in America. It was a long time ago. I spent some time in California and then bought a car and tried to drive it right across the country, Jack Kerouac style. I didn't make it. The car packed up three-quarters of the way across and I had to catch the bus. I had spent a lot of time imagining that journey before I actually undertook it. And now, all these years later, I can remember different places in the mountains and in the desert and the mid-west and so forth. But there's no way of knowing which are the places I really visited and which are the ones I made up in my head. What am I saying? I'm not sure. Something like this: I'd like to know, and you can tell me about it tomorrow afternoon, I'd like to know what you *imagined* the Little Red to be before you went there. If you wrote something or painted something today I would be very happy but you don't have to. I'm interested in the difference between expectations and... I don't want to say reality but you know what I mean. The places in your head. The gap between what is and what might be. That sort of thing.'

Michael walks across the room, finds an unoccupied chair, and sits down. He has finished speaking. He gazes at the psychogeographers, a benign expression on his face indicating his readiness to help and advise when needed.

A general murmuring and milling about ensues. Phil, Doug, Freddie and Esther start preparing materials to carry on with their mixed-media mural that will occupy the whole of the back wall of the room when it's finished. Daniel would like to speak to Val now but she is deep in conversation with Doug and he doesn't feel he can interrupt. He gets out his drawings of Isabel and leafs through them, wondering what to do next.

An hour has passed and Daniel has started making an illustrated diary of the few days he has spent here. He has written a few short sentences and made some line drawings of real and imaginary buildings. He has made a sketch of a real and imaginary person: Isabel, naked, her back to the viewer, walking away and looking over her shoulder as she goes. He covers the drawing over when she comes into the room.

He watches her go to Michael and say a few words, probably apologising for her lateness. She walks across and speaks to Val. She whispers something in her ear and the two of them share a hug and some laughter. Then she moves towards Daniel. She is smiling, the smile fades, a different smile appears to replace it. She stands in front of him and looks at him steadily. Eventually she speaks.

'I'm very happy,' she says. 'Do you want to know why?'

He nods his head.

'Then we need to get away from the others and talk. Can

you bear to do that?'

He nods again. He follows her out of the room, down the stairs and outside. They sit down on the bench near the bottle sculpture. Isabel takes a small white plastic object from her bag and shows it to him.

'I bet you don't know what this is,' she says.

'You're right.'

'It's a pregnancy test. That's what I've been doing this morning, shopping and weeing. It has two possible readings, a *yes* or a *no*. A plus or a minus sign appears in this little window. You see?'

'Yes,' he says, not looking closely, very shocked and painfully uncertain as to what it might mean.

'So you see why I was preoccupied yesterday,' she says. 'That's why it was difficult for me to speak to you. It felt like my whole future was in the balance. But now I know. This morning I've been dodging the showers and dodging the puddles and thinking it through and I'm very happy.'

He can't speak. He waits for her to say more.

'You know there's a right time for this to happen. Every woman wants to have a child when the time is right, every woman I've ever spoken to. The longing grows the more you put it off. Men don't experience anything like that do they?'

'No.'

'So you can't really understand.'

'No, I don't understand.'

'I will have a child one day, Dan, and it will be wonderful. It's something to look forward to. And now I'm very happy. I'm not pregnant and I feel free.'

'You're not pregnant?'

'No.'

'That's good, then,' he says. 'That's very, very good.' He thinks for a while. 'And that's why you were so preoccupied?'

She nods her head.

Daniel does some more thinking. 'If we became lovers,' he says. 'Then one day, I mean one day in the future, not soon. I'm really not in a hurry. But one day...'

'Yes?'

'One day we could have children.'

'We could.'

'Meanwhile, we could spend a lot of time practising.'

'I can't imagine what you mean,' she says, trying to look prim and not succeeding.

'You know. Making love. It would be something to do to pass the time.'

Isabel smiles enthusiastically. 'It's certainly worth thinking about,' she says. Her face takes on an eager expression. 'It would be something to pass the time.'

It is early afternoon. Daniel and Isabel are back at the Gallery again after spending the morning together dodging showers and wandering in and out of bookshops and cafes. They have talked about things both trivial and profound, funny and sad; they have talked about people they know and about themselves. They now refer to their recent momentary difficulty as *the glitch* and believe that it has brought them closer together. But they haven't touched each other. They haven't even held hands. He imagines that their lovemaking, when it happens, will be intense and extraordinary. It will be, as she said, irrevocable.

They walk around the sculpture of a ship's cabin in a

bottle and look in through the portholes. They stand at the water's edge and look across at the city. When it begins to rain they rush into the Gallery to take shelter. They are standing by the front door when Michael comes down the stairs and into the foyer. He seems pleased to see them together.

'How's things?' he asks.

'Fine,' Isabel says. 'We'll take off again when the rain stops. We might go for a ramble.'

'Where to?' Michael asks.

'Where to, Dan?' Isabel redirects the question.

Daniel shrugs his shoulders. 'Somewhere with a view.' He turns to Michael. 'What about the Folly, is that worth a visit?'

'It's OK. It's nothing much unless you can get in and up to the top. It's just a brown stone tower in a sea of suburban housing. Someone forced the door a week ago and I don't think it was fixed properly. If you can get in and don't mind a dodgy staircase leading to a roof with a broken parapet then give it a try. I've been up there. It's OK if you're careful and nobody sees you. You can take the bus.'

'We'll walk,' Isabel says. 'Between showers.'

'I don't know what you'll do if you can't get in,' Michael says. He is silent for a moment, turning something over in his mind. He smiles. 'You might need to shelter from the rain,' he says. He reaches into his pocket and takes out a bunch of keys. He separates one from the bunch and gives it to Isabel.

'My flat,' he says. 'I've got a studio flat up there, I've spoken of it I think. Number sixty-seven, Hamilton Road.' He pauses as if he is working out what to say. 'It's like this... it's... well, it's a studio. It's where I can work away from all distractions, away from the family. But it's also a flat too. I stay up there sometimes. There's a cooker and an electric kettle and a bed and a bathroom and everything. What I want to say is... make yourself at home. If it rains, I mean, and you need to take shelter. Stay there as long as you want.'

'How do we get there?' Isabel asks.

'Fairfield Lane. You follow it up from the roundabout by the canal. It bends back and forth but it gets you to the top of the hill eventually.'

'The Folly it is, then?' Isabel asks, turning to Daniel.

He nods his head and smiles at her. 'Sounds good to me.'

It is not raining but Daniel and Isabel are in Michael's studio flat anyway. They make no pretence about what they have come here to do. They stand in the middle of the second room, the one that isn't full of half-completed paintings and artist's materials but is some sort of living room and bedroom combined.

'OK,' she says. 'I've got you where I want you.' It is a joke and it is serious; her voice crackles with sexual desire.

He laughs, takes her hands, pulls her gently towards him, tries a first tentative kiss. She moves her head to one side and rests it on his shoulder. He touches her hair with his lips.

Now she turns her head and she kisses him. It's urgent and it's intimate; she probes his mouth with her tongue. She rubs her body against his like a cat. Then she slips her hand underneath his T-shirt and presses her fingertips into the muscles of his back, kneading and pinching and scratching.

'It's better like this,' she says. 'Not starting with sex, getting close in other ways first. It's not just about sex, is it?'

He eases himself away from her and laughs. 'No. It seriously isn't,' he says, not sounding at all serious. He pushes her hair to one side so that he can touch his lips against her ear. He runs his fingers around the curve of her arse. 'Not at all.' He pushes at her clothes, brings his mouth against her collarbone for a moment. 'But then again...'

She pulls away from him, turns, and looks at him very seriously. She takes off her clothes, one item at a time, and then watches as he does the same. They move in close, kiss, and rub their naked bodies against one another. Then she moves away from him and quietly lies down on the bed.

He kneels beside her and kisses her mouth, her shoulders, her breasts. He takes one nipple between his lips, and then the other. He lifts her foot and sucks her little toe.

'No,' she says. 'Too tickly.'

He kisses her calves, runs his lips and tongue up the inside of her thighs, gently eases her legs apart.

'Stop now,' she says. 'I hardly know you.'

'We can change that,' he says.

'No.' She smiles down at him. 'It's our first time.'

He kisses the inside of her thighs again, gradually bringing his mouth in closer. She rests one hand on the top of his head and guides his movement. Now his breath and now his lips and tongue touch the place between her legs. He licks her slit, her swollen clitoris. He fucks her with his tongue.

'Yes,' she says.

When he believes that she is ready he moves up and touches his cock against her. He pushes and enters a little way. He holds himself still for a moment.

'Please,' she says.

'Please what?'

'Dan.'

'Yes?'

'Fuck me now. Gently at first.'

He does as she asks, gently at first, and then harder. It is the expression of his love.

The city is mindstuff, Michael once said *one part memory and one part imagination.* Daniel lies on the worst bed in the world, in the worst bedroom in the world, in the house on Paradise Road. It is the afternoon of his fifth day back in the city and he is thinking of Isabel and himself making love. They had walked up the lane together and reached Michael's flat. That much is memory. They didn't go inside and they didn't make love. That never happened. It is something that he can only imagine.

He remembers that she once touched him on the arm to get his attention. She was pointing out something and she touched his bare forearm with the fingertips of her other hand. She said something about being friends. She said *I'm glad you're here.* That was the only physical contact they ever made. It didn't seem significant at the time.

Twenty-six

It is the afternoon of Isabel's fifth day in the city and she doesn't know where she is or where she is going. She is on an unfamiliar street in an ordinary part of town, accompanying Lucy on her way to pick up her son from a friend's house. The sky over their heads is grey and getting greyer; perhaps it will rain soon.

They could have taken the bus but Lucy wanted to walk. Her route is an eccentric zigzag that connects places she once knew. From time to time she starts an anecdote with words like: *I used to live in that house, the one with the green paintwork,* or, *this is the place where I fell off my bike.* They have walked for half an hour without discussing anything serious or deeply personal. It is Isabel who decides to take the plunge.

'I have been thinking about that time when I was here before,' she says. 'I'm not so upset by it now.'

'Good,' Lucy says. She glances sideways at Isabel, doesn't slow her walking pace, waits to hear more.

'I was being a bit daft,' Isabel continues. 'It had become a no-go area.'

'*I don't do memory,* you said.'

'Did I really say that? I've changed my mind. If I'm going to live here then I have to come to terms with that stuff...'

'I guess it was pretty heavy,' Lucy says, filling in the pauses, keeping the conversation going.

'Heavy? No. Well, yes, at the end. That was horrible.' She dries up for a moment. Frowns. Then she is smiling and looking out into some far distance. 'I wouldn't say it was heavy. It was intense. We didn't do anything crazy but the strength of our feelings was very great.'

'Both of you?'

'That's right. I think so. And that was the extraordinary thing, the fact that two people should both feel so much. Of course it was nonsense, in a way. We were so in love but we didn't really know each other, that's daft, isn't it?'

'If you say so.'

'But we shared that feeling. We felt the same and we both knew it. It brought us very close together and it made us separate from everybody else. That is when we finally got around to telling each other. It was on the last day...'

Isabel falls silent for a while. Then she speaks very quietly. 'It would have been so good,' she says.

They walk on without speaking for some time. Lucy brings them out onto a busier road. There is a continuous stream of cars passing in both directions, a few lorries, sometimes a red bus. There are post-war council houses on their left, mock-Tudor semis on their right. The road follows a gentle curve. It begins to climb a hill. Isabel stops and looks at an older building, an ex-farmhouse now engulfed by suburbia. She stares at it for a while in silence.

'It's not for sale,' Lucy says.

'Did it used to be painted white, do you think?' Isabel asks.

'Maybe. I can't remember. I don't come up here that often.'

'Does this road go up to the Folly?'

'Yes, that's right. That's where we're going to pick up Jamie. It's called Fairfield Lane.'

'Fairfield fucking Lane.'

'Iz!'

'I'm sorry. It's just that I've been here before.'

Lucy starts walking again and Isabel is obliged to do the same.

'You had better tell me about it,' Lucy says. 'You're not going to do the I-don't-do-memory thing on me again, are you?'

Isabel laughs. 'There will be a short intermission while I get my thoughts in order. Then, if I can bear it, I'll tell you what happened.'

The road bends back in the other direction and the Folly comes into view. It is a small tower, unimpressive, only half the height again of some of the buildings surrounding it. They carry on walking and it is lost from sight.

'I walked up this road with Dan,' Isabel begins. 'We were on a sort of high, talking a load of nonsense that seemed profoundly important to us at the time. I think we said that whatever happened we would always care for each other. That turned out not to be the case.'

'And what did happen?'

'I think I told you about the other man, the musician. I didn't know but I think I suspected something. Except, of course, that might be hindsight kicking in.'

'Isabel, you're not making much sense.'

'I'm sorry. I really didn't think we would be walking up this road today. It looks different. It seemed a bit brighter and cheerier then, I suppose it was better weather. And we were very happy. But I had some doubts, a sort of paranoia. You know, when everything is going so well and you can't believe it's true. You think it's going to go terribly wrong...'

'And?'

'It went terribly wrong.' She lets out a humourless laugh. 'It was so awful, Lu. I can't believe how much it all went to crap.' She takes a deep breath. 'I had a feeling, something like guilt I suppose. I thought that Max was following us.'

Twenty-seven

Michael stands in the foyer of the Gallery, his eyes on the door that Daniel and Isabel have just closed behind them. His thoughts follow them for a moment; he imagines them walking up Fairfield Lane hand in hand, looking at the Folly, making themselves at home in his flat. But he is also aware that some of the psychogeographers have come down the stairs behind him. He turns to find Phil, Doug, Freddie and Esther standing in a row, waiting for his help. They need spray cans, card for making stencils, masking tape, all sorts of things. It sounds like the mural is really going to take off. He goes to the storeroom and lets them in so they can take what they want. Then they set off upstairs again, talking excitedly. They remind him of children at a birthday party.

Michael feels he should leave them to do their own thing for a while. He goes out of the door and onto the dockside. For a moment, until the rain comes in again, it is a beautiful day. The sunshine makes glossy patterns on the dirty water in front of him. It lights up the city. It is hot enough to make steam rise from the puddles and the wet concrete. He wanders about outside the Gallery, not wanting to go back indoors for a while but keeping close by in case he is needed. He is half in this world, half in the world of dreamy thoughts, when he sees someone he recognises striding towards him, broad smile fixed in place, hand outstretched to grasp his. Michael hears a voice in his head, his own voice, saying *oh shit, not him, not now.* The words that leave his mouth are somewhat different.

'Max,' he says. 'How good to see you again.'

'Fabulous day, isn't it?' Max says. 'I'm always lucky with the weather. Pouring down like mad on the motorway but now I'm here the sun's out. How are you, Michael? How's it all going?'

'Well. Everything's going well. It's been a very good week so far.'

'You look surprised to see me,' Max says. 'And, to tell the truth, I'm rather surprised to be here myself. I had a rehearsal, a small gig, some teaching to do. A busy week. But the gig was cancelled and the person I'm meant to be teaching has fallen ill so I dropped by on my way home. Is Isabel about?'

Michael hesitates for a moment. 'I'm not sure,' he says. 'I don't know where she is. Perhaps she's upstairs. I'll tell you what, I'll come in with you and see if we can find her.'

Michael leads the way into the Gallery and up the stairs to the third floor. He steps into the room ahead of Max.

'I don't suppose anyone knows where Isabel's gone,' he says to the assembled company, scowling at them as he speaks, hoping to make clear what answer they should give.

'No idea, mate,' Phil says, quick on the uptake. 'Sorry about that.'

One or two people shake their heads and then everyone turns back to their work in progress. Except for Doug, who, as a geologist, operates on a different timescale from other people. He now turns away from his corner of the mural and looks across to Michael and Max.

'Didn't they say they were going up to the Folly?' he asks. 'They only set off a few minutes ago, you could...' He becomes aware of the ghastly silence surrounding his words but feels obliged to go on. 'I guess you could catch them up.'

'Isabel and Daniel,' Max says, voicing something between a question and a statement. 'I don't know.' He sounds defeated. 'But I suppose it would be perverse of me to have come all this way and not to make the effort. Someone tell me how you get to the Folly.'

The best part of an hour has gone past since Max set out, on foot, after the lovers. Michael has had nothing to do; everyone present is silently absorbed in their work. He has gone downstairs and out onto the dockside, upstairs again to the third floor, maybe half a dozen times. He cannot make a good guess as to Max's state of mind and he imagines a number of possible scenarios. One possibility: Max never catches up with them, comes back downhearted, drives off into the sunset. Or: he does get within sight of Isabel and Daniel and they are doing... what exactly? Walking hand-in-hand, kissing passionately perhaps. Max will turn away, walk back to his car, and drive off. Michael feels sorry for the man; there was an air of sad resignation beneath the false *bonhomie*. It is quite conceivable that scenario one or scenario two are being played out right now. But there are other possible outcomes; there is something about Max that worries Michael. And he feels in some way responsible.

Michael goes down to the foyer and uses the phone at the front desk to call for a taxi. He goes out, walks along the edge of the docks to the road and stands waiting. Five minutes passes but it feels like half an hour. A cab pulls up beside him and he gets in.

'Folly Hill,' he says. 'Can you drop me off by the Folly?'

He makes a half-hearted attempt to look for Isabel and Daniel on the way up Fairfield Lane but he imagines that they must be near the top of the hill by now. He arrives at the Folly having seen nothing of the lovers or Max. He pays the taxi driver and gets out. The door of the Folly is locked shut and there is no one about so he sets off around the corner in the direction of his flat. And there, right in front of him, walks Max. A hundred yards further on, not far from the junction with Hamilton Road, he can see Isabel and Daniel. Michael follows behind, making no attempt at all to hide from any of them. They seem too caught up in their own business to notice him.

The road they are all walking along ends in a T-junction. Directly opposite is a group of slightly larger houses and on the ground floor of the middle one is Michael's flat; he can see the green front door from where he is now. Isabel and Daniel reach the corner and hesitate; they appear to be lost. They ask a passer-by for directions but he shakes his head; he can't answer their questions. Max, meanwhile, is walking more slowly. Michael wonders if he intends only to watch the lovers, and find out what is going on, rather than confront them. Now Isabel and Daniel have realised that they are in the right street. They cross over and stand outside Michael's house. Isabel takes the key out of her pocket and holds it up for Daniel to see, making it into something symbolic. She passes it to him.

Max has now reached the corner and is only just across the road from them. It seems incredible to Michael that they haven't seen him until he realises that they are, of course, much more preoccupied with each other than with the rest of the world. He walks faster, almost breaking into run, until he comes to a stop a few yards behind Max. He sees what Max sees: a key being turned in a lock, a door being opened, Daniel stepping inside, Isabel following him, the door closing behind them.

There is a small car being driven down the road too fast; Michael hears the high-revving engine, sees it coming towards them. Max does not. Before the door has shut completely Max launches himself into the road. It isn't clear whether the car crashes into him or he crashes into the car; Michael thinks it is the latter. He hears the dull thud of the impact and sees Max fall to the ground. The car doesn't stop. It turns the next corner and is lost from sight. The door opens again.

Max lies on his back, one arm stretched out at an awkward angle. He appears to be unconscious. Michael searches his pockets in the hope that he has for once remembered to carry his mobile. He hasn't. He runs across the street, pushes past Isabel and Daniel and goes into the flat to phone for an ambulance. It takes some time, longer than he could imagine. He goes out onto the street again. A number of people have gathered around already. A man stands in the road and waves his arms to slow any traffic that should come along. Isabel kneels in the road with Max's head in her lap. Michael feels that this is wrong; it doesn't look like a picture from a first aid book. But he doesn't interfere. He looks around for Daniel and sees him standing a few yards away, looking very shaken by what has happened and doing nothing to help.

Michael waits for the ambulance. He watches Isabel stroking Max's head, the side that isn't covered in blood. He is still unconscious but she speaks to him anyway; Michael can hear her words from where he stands on the other side of the street.

'It's going to be OK, sweetheart. You'll be alright. Max, my love, I promise you everything will be alright.'

Michael looks up to see how Daniel is taking this. He sees him turn and walk away down the street. He reaches the corner and passes out of sight without once looking back.

Twenty-eight

Daniel wakes early on his last day in the city. This afternoon the owner of the house will be back, a friend of a friend, someone who Daniel has never met and doesn't feel much like meeting. He needs to be long gone and far away by then. He gets out of bed, dresses hurriedly, goes downstairs to the kitchen. There is still no sign of the cat that he was meant to look after but he puts out fresh food and water for it in case it should turn up. He writes a note explaining the broken window and leaves it on the table. The kitchen is not a nice place to be and he can't face breakfast. He needs to be out of the house for a while.

Daniel leaves by the back door and goes through the tunnel under the railway and into the park. He climbs the low hill and walks along the tarmac path at the top. The weather is dull; heavy clouds, some blue, sunshine and showers both on the way but neither of them here just yet. The path runs level and gives a view of the city on one side and the suburbs on the other. Daniel doesn't look; he has things to think about. He came here for a break from a relationship that he didn't believe in. Now, a few reflective and sometimes lonely days later, he still feels the same. He thinks it is time to make an exit while he can still do so without causing too much hurt. To let things go on longer would be a lazy mistake. There, he has decided; it's saddening but it feels right. He realises that he will miss the little girl more than her mother; he hasn't thought of that before but it's true. And it's even more reason for leaving now rather than later. Meanwhile he should make an effort; he will walk into the centre of town this morning and buy them both a present.

The path begins to run downhill so he turns and walks back. Now he can look at the view of the city spread out to his right. It seems different to him this morning; there is a weekend rather than weekday feeling in the air. He watches a patch of blue sky travelling towards him from the west. If he stays up here for a while it will pass overhead and then, a little later, the sun will come out. He stops walking and stands facing the city, feeling the wind on his skin, waiting for a change in the light.

He thinks of Fairfield Lane, of the showers and patches of sunshine travelling by, of himself and Isabel talking excitedly and lapsing into silences. It was a day very much like this one. Perhaps that is why he hears her voice and these words: *It's going to be alright, Max, my love. I promise you everything will be alright.*

'Fucking shit,' Daniel says out loud. He looks around to see if there is anyone close enough to hear him but it's OK. 'Fucking hell,' he says. 'That hurts.' He starts walking again, more quickly than before. He thinks that he has just been on the receiving end of what is known as a sharp reminder. And it was sharp; it took his breath away. It was a fragment of memory; the moment when she chose the other man and there was nothing he could do but run away. He was right to run, wasn't he? It seemed like the right thing to do for everyone's sake. But mostly it was about not getting hurt too badly. He was running to save himself, he has to admit that now. And with that comes the thought that if he cared for Isabel so much he ought to have stayed around for a while to see if he was needed. When the time was right he could have faded quietly into the background.

The patch of blue has travelled over his head and the sun does come out now, for a while. It lights up the city and he has to stop and look. He lets his eyes travel up and down the traffic-infested roads, over church spires and office blocks, along the stretch of water in the floating harbour, past red cranes and green cranes. The city looks pretty fucking good. He wishes it didn't but it does. The sun is behind him, he can feel it on the back of his head; it throws a warm morning light onto everything he sees. Isabel and he had talked about this more than once, the way the light is richer and everything looks good if you face away from the sun. He thinks that they spoke of it on that last morning as they walked towards the Folly and Michael's flat. He was living in the present then, more intensely alive than at any other time in his life, poised on the brink of the happiest and best experiences of all. And he thinks for a moment that he would give anything to go back there, to a time and place that cannot now exist.

Daniel makes his way to the path that leads back down to Paradise Road. He still can't face breakfast in that kitchen; he will pack his bag, lock the house and get away as quickly as possible. He will go into the centre of town and buy presents and when he feels hungry he will go into one of the cafes on Doubleday Street and get something to eat. He will walk to the bus station and if there isn't one due he will walk to the foot of the motorway and try to hitch, as he did before. He will move on and something new will happen, something unanticipated. He looks forward to it.

Twenty-nine

Isabel's last day in the city. She wakes very early after a bad night's sleep and goes straight to the hospital to see if Max has regained consciousness. The sister takes her to one side and tells her that he is OK, concussed but not badly injured, conscious now, and will probably be allowed to leave tomorrow. He has a headache but will be pleased to see her. She goes to the ward, finds herself a chair and carries it over to sit beside him. He wakes from a shallow sleep and smiles.

'Isabel,' he says. 'It's good to see you.' He puts a special emphasis on his words, as if they carry extra layers of meaning.

'I hear that you're going to be alright,' she says. 'I can't tell you how relieved I am. I didn't sleep much last night.'

'I'm sure you didn't,' he says.

'Because I was worried about you.'

'I know.'

Max wears a bandage around his head, is pale and unshaven, a little weary. But his mental faculties are not impaired; he is his usual self, in command of the situation, speaking with carefully measured irony. He pushes himself up the bed and rearranges his pillows so that he is in a more upright position.

'I'm sorry,' Isabel says.

'What, exactly, are you sorry about?'

'I'm sorry about the accident.'

'Anything else?'

She looks away from him. 'You're in hospital. You're recovering from being hit by a car. This isn't the best time to discuss things.'

'I think it is.'

She turns her face towards him and nods. 'OK,' she says.

'Are you in a relationship with young Daniel?' he asks.

'No.' She hesitates. 'Yes. Yes, I am. We haven't slept together but... but yes, I think we're in a relationship.'

'And where does that leave me? Us?'

'I'm sorry, Max.'

'I understand.'

'I'm still very fond of you.'

'But you're leaving?'

'Yes. I'm sorry, really.'

'Will you please stop saying that you're sorry,' he says, in a quiet, controlled tone of voice.

She nods her head and falls silent. She feels sad on his behalf. She is also aware that she is getting off lightly; here, in a full hospital ward, he cannot show his anger.

'I'm thankful for the good times we've had,' she says.

'Yes,' Max says. His face is without expression, as if he is exercising considerable self-control. 'I too, am grateful for the good times we have had.'

She looks down at his hands on the bedspread and sees they are closing into tight fists. When she looks up into his face again she is surprised to find that he is crying.

'I'm...' She stops herself short.

'Oh, really?' he says, more loudly than he intends. And

then, lowering his voice, 'I think it would be better for both of us if you left now.'

Isabel nods her head, gets up, and walks out of the ward.

Isabel's last day in the city. She lies in the comfortable bed in Erik and Neil's guest room, turning things over in her mind. She is brought into the here and now by the sound of someone knocking on the door.

'Half past eight, Iz.' It is Erik. He opens the door a little way and sticks his head in. 'I've brought you a coffee.' He comes into the room. 'Only Neil's gone and I have to be away soon and I didn't think I'd see you when I got back. Are you awake?'

She laughs. 'Yes, I'm awake. Come in please. Thanks for bringing me coffee.'

He puts the cup on the bedside table and sits down on a chair in the corner of the room. 'And how are you this morning?' he asks.

'OK.' She pulls herself up into a sitting position. 'But not completely OK. I'm going to think about the Little Red Lighthouse and it will make me feel sad.'

'Do you want to be sad on your own or sad in company?'

'In company, please.'

'Good, then you can tell me about it. If you want to.'

'Won't I make you late for work?' she asks.

'I'm alright for a bit. Especially if you need a listener and want to tell a good story. What and where is the Little Red Lighthouse? It sounds like something out of a children's book.'

'The lighthouse, is, was, made of scrap and was one of quite a few sculptures at a municipal tip outside a place called, perhaps, Stanton. Is there somewhere near here called Stanton?'

He nods. 'It's on the way to the estuary. It's not much of a place.'

'It was on the last day of that project. There was a bit of a build up to the non-event. It actually turned out to be about the most traumatic non-event I can think of. Personally, I mean.'

'Is this before or after the accident?'

'The day after. I left Max in the hospital, went to the Gallery and there was a note for me from Michael in case I wanted to follow them and join in the last day. I did want to. I wanted to see Dan.'

'You didn't have a car then, did you?'

She shakes her head. 'There were bicycles at the Gallery. It took me three-quarters of an hour to get there but they hadn't been there long. I hadn't missed much...'

'And you saw Daniel?'

'I spoke to a nice man called Toby and he showed me where everyone was, all standing around talking nonsense, Michael especially. There were the so-called sculptures, things made of scrap. Michael stopped talking and asked me how I was, how Max was. I said he was alright. I kept looking around. I expected Dan to turn up from behind something. To me he was very present, it was just a question of him showing himself. But it didn't happen and nobody would say what was going on. And I didn't want to ask. So they carried on talking complete bollocks, that's what Dan would have thought of it if he had been there, complete bollocks. But he wasn't. And it became obvious that he wasn't going to turn up. No one would say anything and I got worried. Frightened really. I can't imagine feeling someone's absence more strongly.'

'Presence and then absence,' Erik says.

'Yes.' She thinks about it for a moment. 'But mostly absence. That's what I remember most.'

'And did he turn up in the end?'

'No. I never saw him again. And to this day I can't imagine what was on his mind. I will probably never understand why he went off like that.'

She falls silent and Erik doesn't ask any more questions.

After a while she begins again. 'I listened to Michael talking complete shit, mythologising the place as if it was somewhere really important. He talked about real lighthouses and imaginary lighthouses. He talked as if places really mattered, you know, all that psychogeography stuff he was keen on. I wanted to say *places don't matter at all, people matter. It's only people that matter.* But I couldn't speak and he went on with his psychoshit and eventually...' At this point Isabel moves from anger to sadness. She lowers her voice. 'Eventually he said something about what we all imagined the lighthouse to be. And then something about the difference between what was and what might be. He put it something like that. He wanted us to think about that difference. He looked around at us in that way he had. Then he saw me and he looked suddenly crestfallen. I don't know what expression I had on my face but he was badly shaken. And they all turned to look and that's when I began to cry. That was the worst moment. They were all so sympathetic and kind and some-how that made it worse.'

Isabel doesn't cry now. She takes a small sip of coffee. Erik waits patiently for her to say more but she doesn't. He stands up.

'I've really, really got to go soon, Iz. But I don't want to say goodbye now. Can we meet later? You said something about going into the centre.'

'I was going to have a look in the estate agents on Doubleday Street again. I ought to give it one last try.'

'What about a little after eleven o'clock? I'm free then and I'm only at the top of the street in the university buildings. We could meet up if you want.'

She smiles. 'Yes, that would be good.'

'In the new cafe, Primary Colours. Sometime after eleven. Yes?'

'Yes. Go on now, you'll be late.'

He stands up and slips out of the door. She can hear him bustling about the house, using the bathroom. Then he knocks lightly on her door and comes back in.

'I've got to go,' he says. 'But I have a question.'

'Fire away.'

'It's about Daniel.'

'OK.'

'Just this – would you like to meet up with him again sometime or is it better that it all remains in the past? It seems to me that it's unfinished business. You could find out what happened. Would you like to see him again one day?'

She thinks carefully before answering. 'Yes, I think so,' she says. 'Sometimes I think I would like that very much.'

Thirty

Michael is an artist; he is aware of the quality of light. What really changes, he thinks, is how we see things. This morning, for example, the sun comes out from behind the clouds from time to time to illuminate a different piece of the city: some warehouses by the floating harbour; the spire of St Peter's; a group of office blocks; the university buildings on the hill. Each scene is lit with sunshine-after-rain clarity for a moment, until the clouds close in again. He finds this stimulating. It makes him see the world afresh.

He walks along the crest of Folly Hill, looking at the different views appearing in gaps between the buildings. He passes a small park with a children's playground, a number of heavily fortified allotments, a war memorial. He comes to a junction, turns and walks downhill towards the lower-lying part of town. At Canal Street he has to wait for a break in the traffic before he can cross. He steps up onto the footbridge above the canal and looks at the water.

The tide is flooding in beneath him, carrying with it a range of debris: broken pallets, chunks of dirty polystyrene, bits of seaweed, some autumn leaves. A brightly painted oil drum floats up midstream and creeps slowly out of sight beneath the bridge. He steps across to the other side and waits for it to reappear. It doesn't. He goes back but it still isn't visible from there. He looks up and down the canal and sees that all the rubbish has stopped moving; the tide has reached its highest point. He decides to wait until it turns. Meanwhile the sunlight catches the top of the timber sheds by the docks. He looks up at the break in the clouds through which the sun shines. When he looks back down again the oil drum has reappeared and is travelling downstream.

Michael crosses over the canal and walks through a new housing development to the next stretch of water, the floating harbour. He doesn't want to walk past the Gallery; he just doesn't feel like bumping into anyone he knows for the time being. So he turns left and walks along the water's edge for some distance until he comes to a small road bridge. He crosses the water and follows a busy road to the big round-about at the centre of town. He turns up Doubleday Street and goes past the bookshop, the estate agents, the new cafe, and on to the older and less trendy place, The Ferry, where he has arranged to meet Christina.

It is now mid-morning and the cafe is filling up with stressed-out shoppers. Christina is already there, sitting at a small table by the window. He buys a coffee and carries it carefully over to join her. They exchange how-are-yous and brief pleasantries before getting to the real news.

'Tell me about Zoë,' Michael says.

'She's coming home next month. She's had a bad time and wants to be near her parents.'

'Both of us?'

'Yes. She said she's looking forward to seeing you.'

Michael is too busy smiling to speak for a moment. Then he becomes concerned. 'What sort of bad time?' he asks.

'Relationship stuff,' Christina answers him calmly. 'She is young and vulnerable and got into a relationship with a difficult older man. But she has been sensible enough to break it off and now she needs some support.'

'From us?'

'Yes, from us.'

'Is she well?'

'She's fine, physically.'

'And she still has that job with the theatre group?'

'Yes.'

'Did you... what did you say about my illness? Is she worried? I don't want her to be scared.'

'I told her that it isn't as bad as it sounds and that you would be OK for a long time. Decades, perhaps.'

'I think that might be true,' he says. 'I've heard that it can be very slow. But I've been funny about it. I've been doing the head-in-the-sand-thing, trying not to think about it but meanwhile imagining it's worse than it really is.'

'You have to find your own way of dealing with things.'

'Maybe,' he says. 'You know, when I was in hospital I passed a door labelled Department of Anaesthesia. I think I got it mixed up with amnesia. I thought it was the doorway to forgetting. Anaesthesia, amnesia, pretty much the same thing. Whatever it was I thought, yes, I can do with some of that. And that's where I've been much of the time ever since. Not facing up to things.'

'I told Zoë that you and I are good friends,' Christina says.

Michael smiles. He lifts his coffee cup but puts it back down again without drinking. 'Thank you,' he says. 'I appreciate that.'

'I told her that we both loved her.'

'Of course we do.'

'But she needed to know it. There are times in your life when you need to hear it said out loud.'

They fall silent for a while. Michael looks out of the window but if anyone passes by that he should recognise he won't see them; his thoughts have turned inwards. He is thinking how much he respects Christina, more than respects, he admires her really. He thinks that she is kind and wise.

'You know I've tried not to get too excited the last couple of days, since your phone call,' he says. 'I tried not to think too much. But I did. I imagined that Zoë had got pregnant.'

'No.'

'That's good. She's far too young.'

'But one day she will be. She'll drift away from us and then she'll need us again from time to time and one day she will have a baby and you and I will be grandparents.'

'Why are we talking about this?'

'You brought the subject up.'

He looks out of the window for a moment and smiles to himself. 'I knew this was going to be a good day,' he says.

'Don't forget your coffee, Michael.'

He lifts the cup to his mouth, takes a sip, puts it down again. 'It's gone cold. I guess I lost track of time.'

Christina looks at her watch. 'I'll get you another one but I've got to go soon.' She stands, goes across to the counter and returns with a fresh cup. She sits down on the edge of her seat, ready to leave. 'Things aren't so bad, are they?' she says.

'I never said they were.'

'No, but you look pretty miserable sometimes. You don't fool anyone.'

'I feel more positive today.'

'Good,' she says. She gets up. 'I've got to go, Michael. I'll see you next week and we can talk some more.'

He says nothing. She goes to the door and they exchange smiles before she leaves and disappears into the Saturday morning crowds.

Michael sits for a while and stares out of the window. He thinks about Zoë and Christina and about his connection to them. The word *family* comes to mind. And then he finds himself thinking about past, present and future; they all look different to him now. He has been revisiting the past often enough recently, too often perhaps. His relationship with the present has been hit and miss; when he should be in the here and now he finds himself to be quite somewhere else. And he has been avoiding the future; it has been too frightening, a kind of black hole. Now, in a new light, these three places come together and share the same meaning; there is a continuity; there are people who he cares for very much. Today, for a while, despite uncertainty and in contradiction to all the shit and darkness, he will believe that life is worth going on with. What really matters, he thinks, is how we see things.

He finishes his coffee, gets up and leaves. He sets off down Doubleday Street, walking downhill, not limping at all. He turns his head as he passes the other cafe, Primary Colours, and tries to look in. The sun has come out and the window glass is alive with reflected light. He sees cars on the street and people on the pavement, brightly lit buildings, a patch of blue sky. He sees his own reflection. And he imagines that he can see through the window and into the cafe. There, sitting either side of a table, are two people he once knew and some-times remembers. He walks on and thinks of them for a moment. He wonders what they are doing now. He wishes them well, wherever they might be.

About the Author

Richard Collins has been a farm labourer, gardener and estate worker. He has taught practical countryside skills on windy hilltops and creative writing in airless classrooms and enjoyed both. His other novels are *Overland* (2006) and *The Land as Viewed from the Sea* (2004) which was shortlisted for the Whitbread Book Awards and the Welsh Book of the Year. Richard Collins lives in west Wales.

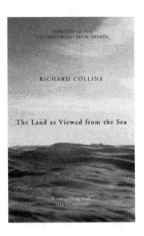

The Land as Viewed from the Sea

Richard Collins' debut novel is a dreamlike meditation on land and sea and the illusory nature of love. Two friends work together on a smallholding: one allows the other to read the novel he is writing, 'The Land as Viewed from the Sea'. As the novel unfolds, fiction begins to intrude upon reality, redefining the friends' relationship, and threatening to change their lives forever.

"Fresh, surprising and ambitious ... Richard Collins' dark-hearted love story is a gripping tale that unfolds with immense narrative skill." – The Whitbread First Novel Award Judges

Overland

Welcome to the happy-go-lucky world of 19-year-old Daniel Brownlow as he travels abroad after leaving school. Things 'just happen' to Dan, a Seventies teenager with a blue Mohican and the nickname 'Madness'.

This rich, deft, second novel again displays Collins' precise imagery of landscape, from Europe's snow-covered mountains to flat roads and cities and down to the coast, revealing the former farm worker's affinity with the land. *Overland* is compulsive: the reader needs to see the book through its unexpected, sometimes enjoyable, sometimes horrific, twists and turns, to its final destination.

Join Seren's Online Book Club

www.serenbooks.com

Join our Online Book Club and get 20% off every book you buy from us. It takes seconds to sign up, with no obligation or charge.

You will also be kept up-to-date with forthcoming titles, news and events. Be the first to know when a new title has been released, see exclusive videos of Seren authors reading from their books and enjoy special offers only available to Book Club Members.

We know readers of Seren titles will be literate, informed and interested in a variety of styles and subjects. We welcome feedback from Members and recognise the value of your comments. Likewise, we want to share our enthusiasm for literature with you. Seren is an independent publisher with a wide-ranging list which includes poetry, fiction, translation, biography, art and history. By joining our Book Club, you'll help us to continue publishing books of high quality and broad appeal.